HAUNTED HOUSE

RICK WOOD

BLOOD SPLATTER PRESS

ABOUT THE AUTHOR

Rick Wood is a British writer born in Cheltenham.

His love for writing came at an early age, as did his battle with mental health. After defeating his demons, he grew up and became a stand-up comedian, then a drama and English teacher, before giving it all up to become a full-time author.

He now lives in Loughborough, where he divides his time between watching horror, reading horror, and writing horror.

Blood Splatter Books
Psycho B*tches
Shutter House
This Book is Full of Bodies
Home Invasion
Haunted House
Woman Scorned
This Book is Full of More Bodies
The Devil's Debt
Perverted Little Freak

Cia Rose
When the World Has Ended
When the End Has Begun
When the Living Have Lost
When the Dead Have Decayed

The Edward King Series
I Have the Sight
Descendant of Hell
An Exorcist Possessed
Blood of Hope
The World Ends Tonight

Anthologies
Twelve Days of Christmas Horror
Twelve Days of Christmas Horror Volume 2
Twelve Days of Christmas Horror Volume 3
Roses Are Red So Is Your Blood

Standalones
When Liberty Dies
The Death Club

ONE WEEK BEFORE LOCKDOWN

CHAPTER ONE

He whistles along to the jubilant tune of *Oh Happy Day* and sings a few words about Jesus washing his sins away and it makes me want to throttle him.

"Can we turn the radio off?" I ask.

"Why? I love this song."

I glare at him.

"Or can we at least turn it down?"

He reaches out and twists the knob. The volume decreases slightly. The sound of the car chugging along becomes audible. I'm not sure which I prefer, his nonsensical whistling along to the song, or the vehicle's reminder that we are officially poor.

Not that you'd know it to look at our new house. But that's where looks can be deceiving. If you were to look at our lavish, grand country home in the middle of endless fields that disappear far into the sunset, you would assume us to be rich. But that house has every penny that we have. We hardly had enough left for me to get my hair cut last week.

"You all right, babe?"

I hate it when he calls me that.

"Fine."

I look out the window. Rest my hand on my chin. Ignore how ridiculously fast he is driving along the outer lane of the motorway.

"This is a good thing," he says. "Really. A new start."

Of course he appreciates a new start. He's the one who was wanked off by his secretary.

Me, I liked the life we lived. London. Busy city. Place I've lived all my life. Friends nearby. Cafes where I can find a table to work at. But there was no way we could both continue this marriage, *and* live where the betrayal took place. It wasn't just Adam and his secretary – it was our friends that knew about it, the job where he was surrounded by women desperate to praise him for being so good at what he does, and the constant reminder everywhere I went that this was the place where my husband was unfaithful.

He's right. If I am to forgive him, we need to relocate to somewhere new. Somewhere in the middle of nowhere. Where I can be secluded. Where I can work. Where his hour-long commute means he's barely home.

Thing is though – I'm not entirely sure I have forgiven him yet.

"You know, there's not much point driving this fast," I say, completely unintentionally. I don't remember making a decision to say it, yet the words come tumbling out of my mouth. "The removal van can't go above sixty on the motorway. We're just going to have to wait once we get there. May as well save the petrol."

"I'm driving, so I'll decide how fast we go."

"You are going to upset the–"

"Hey, babe." I stretch my fingers then curl my hands in to fists. "Remember what Doctor Zhago said? Saying *you* isn't helpful. We need to make *I* statements. Like, 'I feel that…' Then it doesn't seem so accusatory."

We overtake a family. They are smiling. Laughing. What the hell do they have to be so happy about?

"Fine," I say. "I *feel*… that you're being a complete dick."

He rolls his eyes. Like he has some moral high ground because my nastiness was more overt than his.

"That's not helpful, Lisa."

"No, Adam, what's not helpful is you lecturing me on how to talk to my own husband."

"I was just reminding you what–"

"Yeah, well next time you're going to remind me, perhaps do it without that stupid grin. Your ego is so huge I'm surprised it fits in your head."

"Mum, Dad, please stop fighting again!"

I glance in the rear-view mirror. Tilly has her arms crossed.

Poor girl. She's only ten. I was at least twelve when I witnessed my parent's raging arguments.

"We're not fighting," I lie. "We're just discussing."

"No, you're not, you're fighting! Stop it!"

She's a smart girl, which means she's hard to lie to; sometimes there are downsides to having an intelligent daughter.

"She's right, you know," Adam says, shooting me a look, and in this moment – this very moment – I want to launch my fist into his cocky leer and break his stupid, pug-nosed face.

"Oh shut up," I say, really wanting to say *oh fuck you* but aware I shouldn't say such a thing in front of the kids.

Tilly still has her arms folded. Eyebrows narrowed into a frown. It's cute, in a way. Then I recognise that look as the same one her father has, and I suddenly find it repulsive.

I glance at Jack, Tilly's twin brother, in the seat next to her. He is engrossed on his iPad. At least we're not traumatising him at the moment. He hasn't got a clue. He isn't as perceptive as Tilly.

It's remarkable, really, how we can have twins that are so

3

far apart in ability – a girl who always gets top marks, and a boy who languishes in bottom sets.

"Mum and Dad aren't fighting," Adam says to her, and I hate it when he refers to us in third person to the children. They aren't two-years-old anymore, you condescending dick. "Mum and Dad are just talking things through."

I hate how we're lying to her. Surely bullshitting a child will do far worse harm than just being straight with her?

Then again, what truth am I supposed to tell her? "Oh, your father saw it fit to let another woman wrap her perfectly manicured hands around his poorly proportioned penis and rub it until a twenty-miles-per-hour load comes squirting out over the arms she shaved that morning."

A flashback of his justification appears in my mind: him, standing in the bedroom with his arms out saying, "At least I didn't fuck her." Suddenly, the rage intensifies and I hate him all over again.

"Dad's right, we're just talking things through, honey."

I hate myself for saying it.

She doesn't look satisfied, but it ends the conversation, and the journey proceeds in silence. This lovely voyage to our new forever home, condemned to eerie stillness and absent apologies.

Eventually, it's time to come off of the motorway. Adam takes us down the slip road, honking his horn at a car who cuts in front of us.

"What a prick."

"Adam!"

"What?"

"The kids."

"But he is."

"But the kids don't need to know that."

He doesn't protest any further, but I can see it in his eyes. He's seething. He will not let this go. This guy clearly needs to learn how to drive, but Adam won't just shrug it off and carry on with his day – he will ruminate about this. He will tell his father when he calls later. He will bring it up next week when we talk to friends. He will have his arms crossed once he finishes dinner, thinking about how he'd like to teach that guy a lesson.

All because someone, who probably realises how dangerously they drove, cut him up.

After ten minutes or so of A roads, the Satnav takes us onto a country lane. There is not a house in sight, just fields and hills. Everywhere. We have to pull over every now and then so an oncoming tractor can get past; aside from that, we come across no one else.

After at least twenty minutes of me wondering how the removal van is going to get down here, we arrive. And here it is. Just as it was the first time we saw it, and when we made our offer. The driveway is long and shrouded with trees, refusing light from the sun, casting us in shadow as we approach our new home.

It is just as I remember it.

It's a Jacobean manor, and a grade one listed building, and it's remarkable that it's still standing. It's just as one would imagine an old British manor house to be. Large, looming windows. A grand porch. Classical architecture. Surrounded by acres of land where I can work in the summer. A steal really, for the price we paid. I can only imagine what it's going to be like to live amongst the rich history of a manor house, thinking about the lords that used to live there, and the servants that used to work. Even its name implies solitude: *Morosely Manor*. It sounds beautifully dark.

And there's not another soul in sight for miles.

Then my admiration of the house falters as I realise: this is where we are going to be stuck. Together. As a family. With no neighbour to knock on our door and say it's a bit late for us to be shouting.

Adam stops the car. Turns the ignition off.

None of us move.

"Hey, kids," he says. "Why don't you get out and explore? We'll be there in a minute."

The kids rush out of the car, running around the house, sprinting over nearby fields, climbing the trees.

This leaves us alone, and a cold feeling of worry overtakes me. The presence of the kids protected me from war, but I can feel his salvo of words coming.

"There really is no point, Lisa," he says, his voice low-pitched and grave, "in us doing this, if you are not going to make an effort."

"Me? It was you that–"

"Yes, I know what I did. And I am so pleased that you chose to forgive me. But I'm not sure that you have."

I roll my eyes. "What do you want? A medal for acknowledging you did something wrong?"

"If we are going to do this, Lisa" – I hate how he says *Lisa* as if I'm a demon and knowing my name gives him power over me – "if we are going to be happy in this house, you need to move on from what happened. There is no point us continuing this marriage if you are going to keep holding it against me."

He's right.

I know he is.

But I'd die before I ever admitted it.

"Fine. I've forgotten about it. It's all done."

"We came out here to get away. So you'd have somewhere nice to work. Somewhere the kids can run around. A new home we can fill with love."

I came out here so we could live in a house that gave me enough space to get away from you.

"So are we going to do that? Are we going to at least try? Because I really want that. Don't you?"

I look into his eyes. I remember those eyes. They are the ones I used to be so entranced with. The ones I used to stare into as we made love. The ones that I first saw at uni, and knew I wanted to keep seeing for the rest of my life.

The eyes that closed as he kissed another woman.

"I just can't stop thinking about it," I admit, and I feel the sobbing in my voice, and I hate it. I don't want to be that woman. The pathetic, wronged wife, crying because some man upset me. That is not who I am. I am strong, dammit, and I will not let him change that.

But perhaps it's the first real, honest thing I've said in a while, and that's why it upsets me.

Because I finally found a way to tell him the truth.

"What can I do?" he says. "Tell me what I can do to change that. Anything, I'll do it."

I have no idea what he can do to change that. If I knew I'd say.

God, I would say.

But, as it is, I have no idea, so I give the only suggestion I can think of.

"I need time."

"Time?"

"Yes. Time for me to stop thinking about it all the time. Time for me to be able to see you as my husband again."

"I am your husband."

"By law."

"By much more than that."

"I hope so. I hope that's what you are."

He reaches out. Places a hand on the side of my face, strands of my hair falling between his fingers.

"I love you," he says, and he leans in and kisses me.

Then he looks at me. Expecting me to say it back.

7

So I say it.

"I love you, too."

He looks relieved.

"We'll make this work," he says. "I promise."

We remain in silence until the removal van arrives. Adam gets out and unlocks the house so they can unload.

I step out of the car and stare at the house that will either be my home, or my prison – I am yet to discover which.

1939

CHAPTER TWO

L ittle Billy James had only just turned ten-years-old when he was evacuated. The war had begun, and people were panicking, but he was too young to understand any of it, and he was too young to understand why he'd been taken from his mother in London, put on a bus with his class and his teacher, Mr Harding, and taken to the middle of nowhere.

One by one, Billy watched his classmates leave for their new homes, wondering when it would be his turn.

Eventually, after a long day of waiting, Billy was the last one left, and Mr Harding set off for the final house.

It seemed to take longer to get to this house.

The roads twisted and turned, country lanes where there were no other cars, or people, or even animals, which was unusual – as Mummy had promised he would see animals because he would be in the countryside.

He turned to his bag on the seat next to him. Opened it. Took out Percy. A light-brown teddy bear with beady eyes and a warm smile. A present from Mummy. A promise. Given to him with her parting words:

"Though you can't hug me, you can hug Percy. And I

promise, every time you hug him, I will feel it – and I will be hugging you too."

He really missed Mummy. So he hugged the bear. As tightly as he could. Knowing that, somewhere, somehow, Mummy would be feeling it too.

Eventually, the driver directed the bus down a driveway that seemed to never end. Trees hunched over the gravel road like monsters with long, spindly arms. Billy looked up to the sky, which was grey, and saw a few storm clouds.

He'd rarely looked up at the sky in London, but now it seemed so large, so important.

The house came into view. It was huge. Nothing like the small flat he and Mummy lived in – it had big windows and a big door and big shadows.

Mr Harding stepped off the bus and waited for Billy.

"Well?" he said. "Are you getting out then?"

He really didn't want to get out.

"Hurry up, I don't have all day."

Mr Harding looked tired. Billy supposed he would be if he'd been looking after children all day.

Reluctantly, Billy stepped out of the bus, and Mr Harding walked him to the entrance.

The house scared him. He wasn't sure why. It was just so… big… and he was so… small…

He trudged forward, the front door getting bigger and bigger and bigger. Mr Harding curled his fist and knocked three times.

No one answered.

He knocked again, this time a little louder.

Footsteps came from inside the house. Big ones. They sounded like Mummy's footsteps when she was in the kind of mood that Daddy used to call *stroppy.*

A key turned in the lock. A bolt slid to the side. The door swung open, and before him stood an older lady, a fierce grimace on her face that made his entire body shiver. Her hair was grey and chaotic, her skirt was dark beige and frumpy, and she held a rolling pin that she hit repeatedly into her palm.

"What?" she barked.

"Hello, my name is Mr Harding, I am here to drop off your evacuee."

She looked down at the boy.

"Well?" she said. "Can't you introduce yourself? Where are you manners?"

"I'm Billy, Miss."

"Very well." She looked at Mr Harding. "I can take it from here. I will take good care of him."

"Thank you. If you need me for anything, please do–"

"That will not be necessary."

Mr Harding nodded, said, "Very well," and left. The bus would crash on the way home and the impact would kill him instantly. Billy would never see him again.

"Well," she said, looking Billy up and down. "Come on then. Step forward, let's have a look at you."

He stepped toward the doorway. She spread his cheeks and inspected his teeth. Felt his bony arms for biceps. Lifted his hair and looked for – well, he wasn't sure. Lice, maybe?

"Hmm," she said, once she had finished scrutinising. "Well it's far from what I wanted. There's no muscle on you. Your hair is greasy. And you're as skinny as a stick. Did your mother not work you very well?"

Billy wasn't sure what that meant. "I don't know, Miss."

"My name is Mrs Allen, and that is how you will address me."

"Okay."

"Okay, what?"

"Okay, Mrs Allen."

"So would you like to repeat the answer to my question?"

"What question?"

Her eyes narrowed. "You are rather rude, aren't you? My question was – did your mother not work you very well?"

"I don't know, Mrs Allen."

She lifted her head, as if celebrating a small victory, but her sneer did not leave her face. He couldn't imagine her ever smiling. She just didn't look like she was capable of it.

"And what did you bring with you?"

"Just clothes, Mrs Allen."

"Enough clothes? I don't want to be spending my time washing."

"I think so, Mrs Allen."

Her eyes turned to Percy, and her glare intensified even further.

"What is this?" she said.

"It's my bear, Mrs Allen. His name is Percy."

She snatched the bear from him and inspected it.

"How old are you, Billy? Eleven? Twelve?"

"I'm ten, Mrs Allen."

"My late husband was already working at ten years old. He didn't have time for toys."

Billy wasn't sure what to say to that, so he kept quiet.

"Are you not too old for teddy bears?" she asked.

"It's from Mummy. She said that–"

"I don't give a damn what your mother said. You will not be behaving childishly in this house whilst I'm in charge, is that understood?"

"Yes, Mrs Allen."

"And that means no toys that belong to babies."

She dug her fingernails into Percy's neck, pulled, and ripped the head off. She tore through Percy's fur, ripping him apart until he was just wool and stuffing, and pieces of him spread across the porch and floated away in the breeze.

Billy wanted to cry.

But he dare not.

Not in front of Mrs Allen.

"Now get in the house," she said. "Go upstairs and clean yourself up. The bathroom is the first door on the left. And I don't want any grubby hands over my furniture!"

His eyes were welling up. He fought against it with all he had, but tears were accumulating, and he was so scared he was about to cry.

"Is there a problem?" she asked.

"No, Mrs Allen."

"Good. Now hurry up."

He entered the house, and she closed the door behind him, trapping them both inside.

WEEK ONE

CHAPTER THREE

"The coronavirus is the biggest threat this country has faced for decades, and this country is not alone. All over the world, we're seeing the devastating impact of this invisible killer."

It's strange, how our prime minister can talk about the world, yet we can feel so small.

We gather around the television. Boxes fill the corner of the room. Some open. Some not. We are otherwise surrounded by empty space.

Lots and lots of space.

Adam's been busy at work. I've been busy writing my blog and watching the kids. Sometimes I wonder if we'll ever bother opening these boxes, or whether it's just easier not to empty them; if one of us has to move out, then at least we wouldn't have to repack our stuff.

The television's been unpacked, of course. The Sky man is yet to arrive, but we can still pick up Freeview – and a parent without a television is a far braver parent than I.

Adam heard an announcement on the radio on the way home that Boris Johnson will be addressing the nation, and that's why he's forced us all to gather together, insisting that we are about to witness a piece of history. If it weren't for this grave speech, there'd be no reason for us to be in the same room.

"Tonight, I want to update you on the latest steps we're taking to fight the disease and what you can do to help. I want to begin by reminding you why the UK has been taking the approach that we have."

I sit on one side of the sofa with Tilly on my lap. Adam sits on the opposite side with Jack on his lap, though I'm not sure how much Jack understands.

I turn my eyes momentarily from the Prime Minister to Adam, whose eyes are fixed regimentally on the screen. He looks so serious.

I am tempted to reach out my hand and take his. A small act of comfort. Something to remind us that, despite what horrors are occurring around the world, we still have each other.

But I don't.

I wouldn't dare.

I haven't held his hand in months. Maybe even a year.

Touching isn't really something we do anymore.

"Without a huge national effort to halt the growth of this virus, there will come a moment where no health service in the world could possibly cope, because there won't be enough ventilators, enough intensive care beds, enough doctors and nurses."

I was going to be a nurse once.

Back when I first met Adam. I intended to train. Work in hospitals. Help people.

But I kept putting it off and putting it off.

When I fell pregnant, we figured that Adam earned enough money that I didn't need to work. So I abandoned the idea. Stayed home and wrote my blog about living happier lives.

About changing your thinking processes. Meditation. Healthy thoughts. Then the blog took off, so I guess that's what I do now. I write about happiness.

What a hypocrite I am.

"To put it simply, if too many people become seriously unwell at one time, the NHS will be unable to handle it, meaning more people are likely to die."

What will happen if one of us dies?

He'd be gutted. He'd inherit barely anything.

I'd be left alone with the kids, but that's not much different to how it is now.

"From this evening, I must give the British people a very simple instruction. You must stay at home, because it's the critical thing we must do to stop the disease spreading between households. That is why people will only be allowed to leave their home for the following very limited purposes…"

The last pandemic was the Spanish Flu in 1918. People seem to be under the impression that we wouldn't have one now because of our advances in medical care. Those people are idiots. The pandemic in 1918 occurred because people came home from the war and the virus spread between countries. And now our world is more connected than ever.

Personally, I think nature is doing this intentionally.

I don't believe in God. Nor do I believe that there is a conscious thought pattern behind our life on Earth. But I do believe in the power of nature in controlling life. And when one species gets too much, nature culls it.

That's what it's doing now.

Culling.

"You should not be meeting friends. If your friends ask you to meet, you should say no. You should not be meeting family members who do not live in your home."

Jesus.

My only escape from this drudgery at home is an occasional dinner date with a friend, or when I can fob the kids off at the child minder's so I can go for a walk and enjoy an afternoon's solitude.

Now there's nothing but this.

The school will be closed. The kids will be here all the time.

What about Adam and his work? Is it essential?

I don't see how being a solicitor would be essential. But I hope.

His phone rings. He looks at it. "It's work," he tells me, and leaves the room.

Oh, God, please don't be telling him he has to work from home.

Please don't take away the only hours I can bare to be alive without drinking.

"If you don't follow the rules, the police will have the powers to enforce them, including through fines and disturbing gatherings. To ensure compliance with the government's instruction to stay at home, we will immediately close all shops selling non-essential goods."

No shopping.

No friends.

No break.

"No prime minster wants to enact measures like this. I know what the damage and disruption is doing and will do to people's lives, to their businesses and to their jobs."

Do you, though? Do you understand?

How could you? You aren't stuck *here*.

Adam walks in, putting his phone back in his pocket. He smiles. I'm not sure if it's genuine. I used to be able to tell, but not anymore.

"What is it?" I ask, desperate to know if his presence is going to disrupt my life.

"I'll be working from home," he says. "They've told us that

we can't go in. Any meetings with clients will take place over Zoom or over the phone. Courts have been postponed."

I feel my entire body sink into the chair. My upright position fades into a slump.

I try not to let it show.

He actually looks happy, and I can tell what he's thinking.

He's thinking this is an opportunity. A time when we can rally together as a family. He probably has images of us home-schooling the children; standing at the front of the study and delivering perfectly rehearsed skits designed to inspire our next generation.

He's thinking about the time we will spend together. The walks. How we could make use of all these fields that go on and on and on into the distance, all around us.

He's thinking about the support. The way we can begin to rely on each other. How we can get through this together, holding each other tight like we would in a thunderstorm. Maybe he thinks we'll even have sex again. That I will be able to touch him without picturing his secretary's delicate hands wrapped around his cock.

But it's not what I'm thinking about.

I'm thinking about how the one escape I had from him – those seven or eight hours plus a long commute – will be over.

It will be Adam, Adam, Adam.

My marriage will crumble far quicker than it otherwise would.

And the children will be around to see it fall.

"That's great," I say, and I turn back to Boris.

"We will beat the coronavirus, and we will beat it together. Therefore, I urge you at this moment of national emergency to stay at home, protect our NHS, and save lives. Thank you."

And it's over.

The transmission complete.

And life in this house left to continue.

LISA'S LIFE LESSONS BLOG ENTRY 46: A HOME CREATED

My dear readers. My friends. I am now in my new home!

Now I know what you're thinking – how can I cope without the hustle and bustle of London's thriving city life?

Well, quite well in fact.

Of course, I miss the life I had. Shops a minute's walk away. The tube that would take me anywhere. The buzz of people.

But country life is so much better for the soul.

The air here is clean. I feel I can breathe again. And, as I assume you've followed my blog for a while, you'll know that I believe the ability to breathe is crucial for a good mental state.

So I breathe in the fresh air, and I breathe out the fresh air.

And I do so whilst carrying my phone in my new bag, a leather satchel that I bought from *Missies*, which you can buy here (this is an affiliate link.)

Of course, no walk through the country is complete without some good walking boots. My personal preference were these gorgeous, thick, stylistic boots, that I bought from *Seaman's* here (this is an affiliate link.)

Now, remember – are you taking time for you?

It's far easier in the country. There are miles and miles of fields surrounding my house where I come across no one. You can barely tell there is a pandemic where I am. But that may not be the case where you are.

So here are my top tips for staying well during lockdown:

1/ Get up in the morning. Lying in sounds appealing, but you will only feel worse.

2/ Get dressed. This will alter your state of mind quite significantly.

3/ Go out. You're allowed one form of exercise a day – so use it. Staying indoors all day is not good for your mind.

And, when you do go out, be sure to wear a mask, like this one that you can get <u>here</u> from *Sadie's Clothes Wear* (this is an affiliate link):

Stay safe, my friends. And stay well.
    Lisa.

CHAPTER FOUR

I finish the blog entry. Post it. Check the time.

It's 11.45 a.m. I should probably get up. Should put some clothes on. My pyjamas smell.

I suppose the bonus to Adam being here is that he's able to sort the kid's breakfast out, though he was keen to point out to me that this will not be a daily occurrence. Usually I'd work in my office or on the sofa – but once he'd brought me some toast and coffee, I had no reason to get out of bed.

But now I do. It's almost lunchtime and, of course, I will be expected to make the sandwiches.

I wonder why this is. Is it because I'm the wife? Are we living according to such standards? I work too. I may not earn the kind of money Adam does, but writing this blog takes work. This latest post took me a whole twenty minutes to write – plus having to find the affiliate links, that I *always* lose.

I get up. The wardrobe is set up but nothing is in it. I open the nearest boxes and sift through my clothes. I find a dress. A long, flowing one, light blue, one of my favourites, and I place it on the bed.

And I hear someone whispering. So faintly it could just be the wind. From behind me. I turn around to look.

That's when the door opens and the kids burst in.

I could have been getting dressed. Where the hell is Adam?

"Mum!" says Tilly.

"Mummy!" says Jack.

It always perturbs me that he still calls me Mummy. He's ten now. Isn't that a bit old?

They run up to me like they are about to dive on me, wrestle me, take me to the floor. Then they halt. Quite suddenly. Remembering that's what they do with Adam, not me.

Of course not me.

Adam's the fun one.

I'm the one who makes the sandwiches.

"Mum, can we go exploring today?" Tilly asks.

"Maybe."

I have to go to the supermarket. I dread to think what it will be like. I heard on the news that some people are queueing for an hour to get in. But if we want to eat soon, we need food.

Again, why is it my job to go to the supermarket?

"Oh, please, Mummy!"

It's *Mum.*

"Why don't you see if your father will take you?"

"Dad said to ask you," Tilly says. "He says he's got too much work to do."

Of course he does.

Isn't it Saturday?

Or is it Tuesday?

It's so hard to remember out here. Normally I'd be able to tell if it's the weekend from how many people are walking past in suits. Here, nobody walks past. Only rats and vermin.

"But Mum, we're bored."

Jesus. First day of lockdown and it's already started. How long is this going to last? Surely we'll be out of lockdown in the next few weeks? It's just the flu, it can't be that bad.

"I have to go to the supermarket," I say. "You are welcome to come with me."

"But Mum–"

"No buts. Some of us have to get food in. You want to eat, don't you?"

Their excitement fades. They nod.

"Fine," I say. "After the supermarket we'll go for a walk, how's that?"

"Yay!"

"Now go set the table for lunch. I'll be down in half an hour."

They rush out.

Finally.

I find the shower. Turn it on. It churns a few times, then water finally comes out. I put my hand under it, and it's cold. I wait for it to warm up, but it just stays cold.

Did Adam not say the seller was putting in a new shower?

More churning. Pipes that haven't been used in a long time croak in the walls.

Eventually, a few splutters spit out of the shower and hot water arrives. It's still only a little warm. I turn the knob. I hate how it takes so long to figure out a new shower. Shouldn't it be simple? Shouldn't there be some consistency in how they work?

After turning and checking, turning and checking, it's finally hot enough to make my skin turn red.

I lock the bathroom door.

Strip.

Step into the shower.

And, savouring the brief solitude before I return to our

game of happy families, I close my eyes, run my hand down my body, and allow my finger to meet my clitoris.

Men always talk about masturbating. Every comedy panel you watch, there's joke after joke about wanking. Never by a woman, though. It's like it's taboo. And, as pathetic as it is, it turns me on a little.

I picture him. I don't know who he is, but I picture him. His body. His arms. His cock.

I place my other hand inside of me. I picture him and I'm riding him and he's riding me and he's grabbing my breasts. We're in a field, I think. Somewhere outdoors. It's sunny, but we're alone. He has long hair. That's strange, as I don't like long hair on a guy. But he has it.

And I can feel his cock. I can feel it in me. I moan as he enters me, further, deeper, in and out, slowly. It's romantic. Adam always fucked me like he was angry. Not this man. This man fucks me like he loves me.

And I feel that twinge.

The one that says I'm close.

I'm about to cum.

A parade of fists shake the bathroom door.

"Mum! Mum! Jack took my toy! He won't give it back!"

And I don't cum.

I drop my hand. Close my eyes. Bow my head. Let the water scald my neck.

"Mum!"

"Go tell your father!"

Heavy footsteps stomp away.

I contemplate finishing, but the moment's over.

The moment is always over.

I wash my hair. Wash my body. Step out. Towel dry. Wrap the towel around myself. Step into the bedroom.

From another box I find a clean bra. Pants. I put them on. Turn to the bed.

My dress isn't there.

How strange.

I could have sworn I'd left it here. Where could it be?

I check the floor. Under the bed; maybe it slid down and went under there. Could Adam have moved it? Maybe the kids jumped on the bed when they came in and knocked it off.

It's not there.

I turn back to the box I took it from. Open it. And there it is.

My favourite dress. Long, flowing. Light blue.

In the box, like it has been packed.

Adam must have moved it. Assumed I was making a mess. Assumed I was just putting a dress on the bed to add to the dysfunction of this household, rather than because, God knows, I might have put it there to wear it when I get out of the shower.

His obsessive tidiness was something I thought I'd love. That we'd always have a clean home.

As it turned out, it's something I hate.

I put on the dress. Go to make sandwiches.

Like I did yesterday, and will probably do again tomorrow.

CHAPTER FIVE

Having been used to all shops and amenities being within a ten-minute walk, it is quite a shock to discover how long it takes me to get to the supermarket.

After what feels like all afternoon driving down a country lane, having to stop only once for a tractor that was already struggling to fit on the road – I had to take the car onto the verge and brush against the bush which, being a people carrier and not some jeep, the car is not used to doing – I arrive onto a real road some twenty-odd minutes later.

Another ten minutes and my intermittent Satnav brings me to a stop at a supermarket, and I park my car between a muddy van and a muddy Nissan Almera. My car must look like the rose between two thorns.

I step out, collecting my bags-for-life. I don't recognise the brand of the supermarket. It certainly isn't one of the big ones.

I go to collect a trolly, but that's not as easy as one would think. There is a bloke, so young he still has pimples, wearing a mask and sanitising all trolleys before we are allowed to take them. It's like a military operation how he gives them to people who are 'socially distanced' – the new term for staying away from each other. I then have to join a queue, where we are all at least two metres apart, and wait a further forty minutes until some bloke with no hair and the skin of a walrus lets me in.

Everyone here looks weird.

There's nobody wearing suits, like in London. There's no pace to people's movements, no hostility in people's eyes. In fact, those without masks smile at me. Most people look old, but they probably aren't. There's a lot of missing teeth and a lot of grubby jeans.

Where the hell am I?

I do the shopping quickly, not lingering long enough in one aisle to pick up someone's body odour or to let someone think I'm willing to engage in conversation.

When I arrive at the checkout – which I have to queue for, two metres apart, up the toilet paper aisle – the young lady is beaming at me.

"All right there," she says, her country accent dripping from her words. "Are you all right with your packing?"

"Fine, thanks."

I hope this will appease her, but, after passing just a handful of items through the scanner, she turns to me and asks, "So what are you up to today?"

"Oh, not much," I say, though I'm tempted to answer *I'm in the supermarket, what does it look like?*

"Just doing a bit of shopping?"

"Yep."

"It's all a bit strange, isn't it? All the queueing and that."

"I guess so."

"Yeah, we're going to do the shopping after I finish. I'm dreading it. So stressful."

"Mm."

There is a gap in conversation, and I hope she's taken my monosyllabic replies as a hint that I do not wish to engage.

She has not.

"So do you live around here?"

I hurriedly pack the last bag.

"How much?" I ask.

She answers. I pay. I leave.

On the radio, they discuss the state Italy is in. They predict things are going to get just as bad here. Surely not. We're in lockdown. We should be back to normal by Easter.

Unfortunately, I don't get to hear the end of the discussion, as all the radio stations turn to static when I get within fifteen minutes of home. I don't even notice, and drive home to white noise.

The kids rush up to me when I arrive, excited, asking if we're going for a walk yet. I tell them to help with the shopping.

Adam shouts hello from the office – the only room that is completely unpacked and set up. He doesn't come out.

I consider doing another post on the blog. If I schedule one for tomorrow then I can have that afternoon off.

"Mum?" Tilly says.

"What is it, darling?"

I rub my eyes. Why am I so tired all the time? Is it just what it is to be an adult – a permanent state of tiredness?

"Are we going for a walk?"

"Yes. Once I've finished unpacking the shopping."

"Do you think we'll find any animals?"

"Maybe."

"I hope so."

I place the eggs in the fridge and turn around. Something catches my eye. Something on the wall.

A photo.

It's black and white. A woman, quite a bit older, stands there. A boy next to her. I take it off the wall and examine it.

I didn't put this up.

Was this here when we moved in?

I turn it over. Written in pencil is the date *September 1939.*
1939?

How has this been hanging here for eighty-one years and
the previous occupants never removed it?

Then I see something else. On the wall where the picture
was. More writing in pencil:

Do not remove photo, for grave peril will subsequently befall.

"Grave peril will subsequently befall…" I mutter. Who talks
like that?

My pencil case is on the table. I rub out the writing. Then I
remove the photograph, but keep the frame – it's still in good
condition, and we could use it.

I walk over to the bin. Go to drop the photo in.

Pause.

Was this the previous owner of the house?

Maybe I should keep the photo. It would be good to learn
about the history of our home. Perhaps it would be worth
keeping.

But there's something more.

A reason I'm not throwing it away that I can't quite articulate. That I don't quite understand.

Something pulls me to this photo.

This woman…

Her name is Mrs Allen.

Of course, I have no way of knowing that. I don't even
know if it's true. It's just a thought I have. An instinct. And no
way to find out if I'm right.

Then again, it doesn't really matter, does it?

"Mum, can we go now?"

This woman. She doesn't smile.

Not just in this photo, but at all other times – her face
looks incapable of it. Like a smile would be an abomination.

A smile *is* an abomination.

She serves the Lord and her husband, and that's it.

I serve the Lord and my husband, and that's it.

"Mum, can we go?"

And this child who stands beside her – he does not deserve my pity. Or my help. He has come to her because he was sent by circumstance, and his mother was too nourishing, too kind, and whilst he's here, whilst this war rages on, this boy is going to learn the true meaning of hard work – and he will be silent and compliant in doing so.

"Mum?"

What an insolent thing a child is.

So rash. So cocky.

No idea about the world.

Too much love makes a child soft.

And this child deserves none of it.

"Mum!"

A glass of water on the kitchen table explodes of its own accord.

"What?" I snap, turning my head around, casting my glare on the child, an intense rage coursing through my blood, like adrenaline only more intense. "What the fuck do you want, you inbred piece of shit?"

Tilly cries.

Why is she crying?

There are tears in her eyes.

Has someone made her cry?

Was it Jack?

No.

It was me.

How was it me?

Oh, God, what did I just say…

I shove the picture in the drawer. Rush to my knees in front of Tilly. She flinches away, but I take hold of her arms and look deep into her eyes.

"I'm so sorry!" I tell her. "I am so, so sorry! I don't know – I don't know what came over me…"

"I'm sorry, Mum. We don't have to go on a walk. I can just play here."

"No, we'll go on a walk. We will. I promise. We'll have a really lovely walk, see if we can find some animals. Yeah? Would you like that?"

I can feel tears in my eyes matching hers.

How could I be so callous?

I can be really wretched sometimes.

But I never thought I'd speak to my child like that…

I wrap my arms around her. Squeeze. Show her as much love as I can.

"I'm so sorry," I repeat, over and over. "I am so sorry, I am so sorry, I am so sorry."

She's still crying, but its lessening. Just sobs.

"Go get your shoes on, yeah?" I tell her. "Go on. And we'll go now. And get your brother."

"Okay," she says, and runs away.

Leaving me standing there. Watching her go.

I glance at the drawer that stores the photograph.

What on earth just came over me?

CHAPTER SIX

I caught the headlines on the television before we set off. They are saying the Prince of Wales is in hospital. They say it might be Covid-19. Which, in a way, really brings it home how catastrophic this all is. Normally, when the world sees catastrophe, it's the poor who suffer. When the rich aren't immune, that's when you know things are getting really bad.

Tilly and Jack love the space. We set off in a field, and twenty minutes later we've crossed it and we're into another field, and this happens over and over. We climb a hill, and from its peak we can see even more fields. In the distance, there are houses. Homes that feel tiny compared to ours.

And the whole time we are walking, those two children do not stop running.

At one point they are chasing each other, at another point they are playing tag, at another point they are just running.

And hey, why not?

They are young. They have the energy. At my age, I only run if I'm being chased, but for them, they have the sprightliness to burst across the field.

Occasionally, I get this strange feeling like I'm being

watched. I keep turning around, but there's no one there. It's just fields. No place anyone could hide.

We come to a small stream. The sun reflects in the water with a beauty only nature provides, and I start to think maybe country life isn't too bad after all.

"Mummy! Tilly! I've found something!"

Jack is halfway across the field, by a wooden stile. Tilly sprints toward him to see what it is and they both gather around something – not touching it, but both enthused about it.

Eventually, I catch up with them, and peer over their shoulders.

"What is it?" Jack asks.

"It's a frog, dummy," Tilly says.

"Don't call me a dummy!"

Sure enough, there is a little frog. But it's not moving. Not running away. In fact, it looks like it's shivering – if a frog can even shiver.

Drown it.

"It's hurt, Mum."

Tilly points to its leg. She is so very astute. Sure enough, its leg is a little crooked.

I feel I'm being stared at again.

Drown it, now.

I keep hearing whispers on the wind. Something faint and distant. I shake myself out of it. It's what brains do; they find patterns in things. They see faces in smoke and hear words on the wind. It's just my mind misinterpreting a gentle breeze.

"Can we save it?" Jack asks.

"I think it's best to just leave it," I say, not wanting them handling a frog. God knows what diseases it might have.

"But Mum, if we leave it here it might die," Tilly protests. "Doesn't it need water to live?"

Drown it, Lisa.

39

I don't know. I feel like this is something I should know. Frogs are often found by water, but is it essential for their survival?

"What if we take it back to the river?" Jack suggests.

"Yes!" Tilly says.

"But I don't want to touch it."

Drown it now, Lisa.

The whispering persists, yet I can't feel a breeze.

"Just leave it," I say, pushing away an odd thought that keeps niggling at me. "I don't want to touch it either."

"I'll do it," Tilly says.

"No, you don't want to–"

But, before I can change her mind, Tilly has swept the frog onto the palm of one hand, then cupped the other over it. She walks with more caution and balance than I've ever seen her walk before, directing herself toward the stream, with Jack and myself following.

When she reaches the water, she gently lowers herself to her knees, reaches her arm out, and places the frog on the bank.

"There you go," she whispers. "You're safe now."

There's still time to drown it.

It hops away, not quite moving right, but evidently more confident now it's near the water.

And I wonder what would happen if it drowned.

"Can we go home now?" Jack says. "I'm getting tired."

"I'm not surprised. Come on then."

The sun is descending, and the bright summer's day is fading to a warm summer's evening. As much as I don't particularly want to return home, we must. Besides, Adam is insisting that we join in with this nationwide thing at eight, where the whole country is stepping out of their front door and clapping the NHS workers.

I'm all for it, except... there's no one around. They are hardly going to know if we clap, are they?

But Adam insisted that it would be good for the kids to show appreciation, even if no one is around to hear it. God knows I don't want another endless argument with him where neither of us budge, so like most days, I just acquiesce to his stubborn requests in my endeavour for an easier life.

We arrive home fortyish minutes later. When we do, my gaze is drawn to something behind the house. Something at the end of the back garden. A small structure.

Is that a well?

And how have I not noticed it already?

Go look at it.

"You go in and wash your hands," I tell the kids, and they do so, leaving me to wander across the back garden – though back garden is a loose term, considering we have acres of fields all around the house, some of which are technically ours. God knows how it works. I didn't really care enough to ask.

As I walk closer, it becomes clearer. It is a well. A circular brick structure surrounded by a circle of bricks to stand on – the only surface I've found near the house that isn't grass.

I reach it.

Look inside.

It's not too deep, but deep enough that one wouldn't be able to climb out. It looks like it has dried up.

Look further.

I peer further over.

It's not that exciting. I'm not even sure if we could use it if it hadn't run dry – the bottom of the well is filled with rubble.

Does it just collect rainwater now? And in that case, I'm not sure rainwater is too hygienic. That's why we have a water supply instead.

I turn around to leave, but something draws me back.

Look again.

A feeling. A niggling thought. Something pulling me to that well, making me want to return to it.

I don't know why, but I obey.

And when I look over, I see a body in the well. A boy. Screaming for dear life.

I panic. Look over my shoulder, but everyone is too far to call. I turn to talk to the boy.

But he's no longer there.

Just rainwater and leaves.

"Hello?" I call out.

My voice echoes around it.

There's no one down there.

I don't know what I saw. It was just my imagination.

It was real, Lisa.

I shake my head. I think I'm tired. My legs are aching from all that walking.

I return to the house to make tea.

LISA'S LIFE LESSONS BLOG ENTRY 47: THE WELL

As you may be aware, I have recently moved to the country. This is something many city people resist, but it is so good for the mind – to be able to walk freely through open fields and not come across anyone else for miles.

What I've discovered, that I didn't realise about here, is a well. It is at the end of our garden.

(This picture is sponsored by *Brian's Books*, your one-stop shop for your next read. Find out more <u>here</u> – this is an affiliate link.)

I did some research, and wells were first used in the Neolithic era – around 7,000 BC.

Although I am sure this well is not that old, I am curious as to when this well may have been created. I believe it is a dug well, as it is made out of brick, but I'm not quite sure what this means.

If anyone has any answers, please do contact me – I would be most interested to learn.

CHAPTER SEVEN

I t's that time I dread.

Bedtime.

It's when Adam talks to me.

We used to use bedtime a lot.

I mean, before.

We used it to talk about the kids, what they were up to, what we'd done with our day. Any grievances we had, or anything we wanted to thank the other person for doing – this was the time we'd do it. Then we'd wait until we were sure the children were asleep, and we'd have sex.

Only problem is, Adam still thinks this is our night-time routine. He seems to forget what he's done, and the space I require from him to heal.

I have been tempted to suggest we sleep in separate bedrooms. But I have neither the guts to do so, nor would I want the children to see just how bad our marriage has become.

I spend longer in the bathroom than I need to. Sitting on the toilet, even though I don't need to go. Being more thorough rubbing cream on my face. Having a few cups of water. A few extra swigs of the mouthwash.

Until I have no choice but to leave the ensuite and enter the bedroom.

"Hey, honey," Adam says. He was reading a book, but now he puts it down. He's lifted the duvet back for me to get in.

"Hi," I say, force a smile, then climb into my side of the bed.

"How's your day been?"

"Fine."

"Did you have a nice walk?"

"Yep."

"Tilly said something about a toad."

"It was a frog."

"What's the difference?"

"I – I don't know. How would I know?"

"I just thought–"

"Just leave it."

I take out my phone. Look at my blog stats. Which is pointless – I can only get a signal in the kitchen, and I've been having to do all my posts from there. When are we getting the damn Wi-Fi?

"Honey?" he says, staring at me.

"Yep?" I don't look at him.

"When are we going to actually talk again? I mean, like humans?"

This is exactly why I took so long in the bathroom. Why I hate this time of day. Why I avoid being alone in a room with him.

Because I act distant, and he calls me on it.

I need time. I need space. And he doesn't get that. He just wants answers all the time. He wants to know why I'm so distant. Why I'm so cold.

Why the hell do you think it is, Adam?

Why don't you take a guess?

"I am talking like a human," I say.

"You're not even looking at me."

"I don't want to."

"We haven't had sex in months."

"I don't want to."

"Why not? I mean, there's only so much waiting a guy can do."

Now I do look at him. "Oh, so you mean if I don't give you any sex then you're going to run off to your secretary again?"

I hold his eyes. He huffs. I've got him.

"That's not what I mean," he insists.

"Then what do you mean?"

"I can't even touch you."

"You can touch me if you want."

He puts his hand on my arm. I flinch. He doesn't remove it.

"See? I touch you, and your body recoils away from me. What is it going to take for you to forgive me and move on?"

I shrug. I try to answer, but I don't have one.

"I love you," he says.

I go to say it back, but somehow the words don't meet my lips.

I hate this conversation. I hate this moment. I hate all of it, and I want it to stop.

"Maybe we should get more marriage counselling or something. Or we should find a new way to talk. 'I statements' and all that. Anything to make us *us* again."

I really wish he would stop talking.

I don't want to hear it. I've heard it before, and the words are so repetitive, they go on and on and on and on.

"If there was something I could do, some way I could change what I did, some way I could make it better, then–"

"You know what," I interrupt. "Why don't we have sex."

I don't want to. God, I don't want to.

But I would far rather watch him heave over me for five

minutes than have him carry on lecturing me, and this is the only way I can think to make him stop.

"Are you sure?" he asks.

"Yep."

"Because you look kind of angry about it."

"I'm not angry."

"Really, because you–"

"I said I'm not angry."

I force a smile. I know it's disingenuous. I know he knows it's disingenuous. But I'm hoping it's enough to just make him get on with it.

"Really, I would just like you to do it now. Please."

"Well, if you really think you're ready then–"

"I am. Hurry up."

He smiles. It's a weak smile.

"Okay."

He lifts the covers and begins moving beneath them.

I suddenly realise what he's about to do.

"No," I say. "I don't need that. Please, just... do it."

"But I kinda need some..."

I look at him. I realise what he's saying.

I huff as I go under the covers and pull down his pyjama bottoms.

There it is.

His penis. The one that his secretary gripped. The one she rubbed so hard it made his cum fire out and drip down her hand.

The one I have done this to so many times before, yet hate myself for doing it now.

I take it in my mouth until it's hard. I wait for him to be ready. After a few minutes, he is, so I lay on my back.

He pulls down my trousers and enters me.

He doesn't even bother taking off the rest of my clothes.

He tries looking me in the eyes. I just want to stare at the ceiling and wait for it to be done, but he's staring at me. I stare back. Awkwardly. Each thrust feeling as uncomfortable as the last.

After a few minutes he goes to move.

"What are you doing?" I ask.

"I thought you'd like to go on top."

I used to love going on top.

"No, just… carry on like this."

"Do you want me to hold off until you're–"

"No, just do it."

He stays in this position and keeps going. It doesn't take long until his breathing is heavy and he's making those noises.

The same ones his secretary would have heard.

I feel him explode inside of me. It's a little painful. I'm not used to it.

When he's done, he stays inside of me. He used to do this. Wait until he was limp; until we were done gazing into each other's eyes.

But right now, I'm desperate to clean him off of me.

So I kiss him to appease him. Then I gently roll him onto his back, and get out of bed, aware that only my bottom half is exposed, and I look stupid.

"Where are you going?"

He's dripping down my leg.

"Just washing myself."

When I'm done, he's still there. Waiting for me. Wanting to cuddle.

"I'm just going to read, if that's okay," I say.

"Okay, but cuddle up to me once you're done."

"I will."

I stare at the same page of my book until I hear him snore. Then I turn out the light, roll onto my side, and close my eyes.

CHAPTER EIGHT

I'm standing over the well.

There's someone with me, but I don't know who she is. She's looking right at me, and I'm looking back, but I could not tell you about a single feature of her face. There is not a part I can comprehend.

The water is full. Overflowing, almost.

She says it's from the storm, but I don't hear her say it.

She tells me to put my head in it, but no words come from her mouth. But she says it.

So I do it.

I put my head under.

And a hand holds it there.

It is my hand, not hers.

My own hand is pushing my head further and further into the water. I am suffocating and I struggle to breathe and I struggle against the arm, but my arm is too strong, I am pushing myself under with too much force.

I finally force my head out of the water and my own scream wakes me up.

I am alone in the bedroom. Sunlight pours in through the

open curtains. I can hear my family downstairs, and I can hear the radio telling me that 1,019 people have now died from Coronavirus.

The time is 9.32 a.m.

I'm normally up at 8.00 a.m.

I'm exhausted. Sweaty. My pyjamas stick to me. I don't know why.

No one in my family thought to come and wake me.

I get up and go in the shower. I masturbate, get dressed, and go downstairs, where Adam has already begun home-schooling. He tells me to take over when I arrive as he has work to do.

I don't seem to get any choice in the matter.

We have nothing for them to do. No workbooks or anything. I am able to access the internet from my phone with weak signal if I hold it high enough in the kitchen, which allows me to find an email with tasks their teachers have sent.

They've provided a website the kids can use to complete maths challenges. That'll do. I send it to their iPads, connect their iPads to my iPhone's hotspot, balance my iPhone precariously on top of the kitchen cupboard, and watch their disgruntled faces as they get aggravated at how long the website takes to load.

"It's the best we can do, you'll have to be patient," I say, knowing that if I was having to do maths challenges on internet sites that took half a minute to load, I would be repeatedly smashing the iPad against the table.

I try to think what to do with them once they've finished these maths challenges. Physical Education, maybe? Get them to play football in the garden?

Gosh, what if I have to check their answers to these maths challenges? I've watched *Are You Smarter Than a Ten-Year-Old,* and I've had a go at answering the questions ten-year-olds have to answer on their tests – and I hadn't a clue.

Surely the website will work out if they've given the correct answers or not.

I have another email through. It was sent ten minutes ago but my iPhone has only just picked it up. Not wanting to take my iPhone from the top of the cupboard where I've left it to get the most signal, I climb upon a chair to read my email, and think about how pathetic this is.

The email has some English assignments for them to do in the afternoon. Some resources they can use to do some kind of creative writing. Hopefully that will keep them busy.

They seem to be engrossed in their gruelling tasks, so I make myself a coffee and retreat to the living room.

I was going to write another blog post, but I dare not connect my laptop to my hotspot for fear that I slow down the websites that are keeping the twins occupied, so I put on the television, the volume low, and it occurs to me just how isolated we are.

If we had a problem, how long exactly would it take for the emergency services to get here? If we were even able to get enough signal to phone them, that is. If one of us were to have a heart attack, there's no way the ambulance would arrive in time to revive us. Apparently the man from Sky isn't even allowed inside my house to set up Wi-Fi. I can't even phone my family, the signal is so weak.

This pandemic could wipe out the entire country, and there's no way that we would know about it.

We are completely and utterly isolated.

And I have never felt more alone.

I flick over to the news. Boris Johnson now has Coronavirus. The Prime Minister, who we're relying on to see us through this mess, is now in intensive care.

How the hell are the rest of us supposed to feel safe when the one who's supposed to protect us becomes ill?

I imagine that's how the kids would feel, should anything happen to me and Adam. Abandoned and helpless.

It's hard to hold onto hope in times like this.

I consider seeing what's on Comedy Central, something to cheer myself up, then I remember that we don't have those channels yet. We can't even pick up half the Freeview channels.

So I sit and watch as the news reporter updates me on just how bleak our lives have become.

And I feel disconnected from every other person on the planet.

LISA'S LIFE LESSONS BLOG ENTRY 48: HOLDING ON TO HOPE

We are all saddened to hear the news about our prime minister.

I am in no way a Conservative voter. I despise them and all they stand for. But this is wartime. We may not have agreed with Churchill's views – heck, the man was evidently racist, albeit in a way that was accepted at the time – but views on wealth are irrelevant at a time like this. When it comes to seeing us through war, we need a leader.

I guess it's hard not to become disillusioned at times like this, but remember that you get through this by being grateful for the small things you have. Your family. Your home. And, hopefully, your health.

For me, I find hope in little things such as this foot massager, which is just £99.99 at *Little Richard's*, which you can find <u>here</u> (this is an affiliate link):

I hold onto my children. I am grateful for them.

I sit with them in the garden, smelling the flowers, feeling the breeze in my hair, and knowing that we live a precarious existence.

But this is what we live for.

And I love my children, I do. Yes, sometimes I may wish to drown them. Throw them in the well and hear them scream. That's what she keeps telling me to do, after all, and she's very wise. But I adore them, I truly do.

And it's important to keep them busy, and keep their education up, such as through these educational worksheets which can be found here at *Karl's Books* (this is an affiliate link):

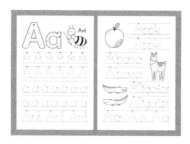

So today, what I would like you to do, is take a moment. Just sit still, no phone in your lap, no noises to distract you.

And I would like you to think about what you are grateful for.

What do you have in your life that you are desperate to hold onto?

And I would like you to write them down. Three things.

And, should you wish, you could use this notebook from *The Stationary Cupboard* that can be found <u>here</u> (this is an affiliate link):

Stay safe, my friends.

And stay strong.

CHAPTER NINE

It's the afternoon. Sun is high. Hot. Really hot. So hot I take my jacket off.

I'm wearing a dress. Flowers on it. Not real ones, just pictures. They don't smell like flowers, they just smell like me, but they are beautiful nonetheless.

I asked Adam what he thinks. He said it's lovely. He didn't look up. He was doing work.

He's always doing work.

Tilly and Jack are running around. Chasing a football. Playing with the portable goal.

I'm stood. Still. Watching.

Watching my children run. Dance.

Dance, little children, dance.

And they notice the well. And they run over to it.

And I hear screaming.

It's not real screaming. No one else can hear it. Somehow, I know that. It's just me.

But it's screaming.

A boy. Young. Maybe a little older than Jack, but not by much.

And his screams come from the well.

They peer over the well.

They could fall in.

They could so easily fall in.

I could push them.

What if I did?

Then they'd drown.

But I don't want them to drown.

Don't you?

They are my children. I love them.

You'd be saving them.

How?

From becoming the adults they'll become.

They might be good adults.

No child ever becomes a good adult. The rot just grows with their bodies.

I rush toward them.

They are leaning over the well. Looking in. Peering in.

The boy's still screaming.

His voice echoes around the well.

Push them.

I'm running now.

Running toward them.

Running toward my children, gathered over the well, peering in at the boy whose screams they can't hear.

Push them in.

It's not safe.

Gosh, it's not safe.

The well is just not safe.

Drown them.

I'm running harder now. My bare feet on the grass. It tickles my soles. It's soft and hard at the same time.

And I reach them.

And I grab them.

And I pull them back.

"What are you doing?" I shout.

They are surprised. Taken aback. Flummoxed.

"You could have fallen in!"

They are upset.

"Get inside," I tell them.

They turn and walk. Quickly. Moping. Back to the house.

I turn to the well.

I still hear the screaming, but when I peer over, I don't see the boy.

But just because I don't see the boy, it doesn't mean he isn't there.

He's always there.

And eventually the screaming stops.

The water fills his lungs.

And he is silent.

1939

CHAPTER TEN

Billy had never heard of a well before, never mind seen one. He didn't know what they were, and Mrs Allen didn't seem to like explaining.

"It used to provide water," she snapped.

"Water?"

"Yes, you know, that wet thing we drink?"

Billy knew what water was, but he daren't say that. Sometimes, Mrs Allen would ask questions to which she did not want an answer.

"I mean, really, what is your mother teaching you?" Mrs Allen grumbled. "Never had to work a day in your life. Men a few years older than you are fighting for our liberty, and you are creating a fuss about a well. Why, when I was a child, I was taught the meaning of hard work. I would have never been so insolent…"

They reached the well.

Mrs Allen turned to look at him. Her eyebrows narrowed even further, and her scowl became all the more intense. With the chaos of her matted grey hair, she looked like she'd escaped from a lunatic asylum.

Billy wished he could go home. He missed Mummy.

"Did you want me to fetch water from the well, Mrs Allen?"

"No, you daft ingrate. This well dried up long ago. The stream doesn't even bring water to it anymore."

Billy felt like saying that, if the well doesn't get water anymore, what was the point of having one?

But he did what he did most days – remained silent.

"Come here," she instructed, and he followed her into the shed where he found a large tub. It was like a water butt, but bigger, almost the size of the shed.

"See this?" she said.

"Yes."

"I would like you to fill it to the top with rocks and stones."

"With rocks and stones? Where from?"

"Do I really have to repeat everything I say?"He stared up at her gormlessly, so she repeated, enunciating each syllable with as much spite as she could, "You. Fill. It. Up. With. Rocks. And. Stones. From. The. Garden."

Billy looked around. The garden was mostly grass, but he supposed he could find some rocks and stones. But enough to fill the large tub? He wasn't sure he could find that many.

"Now!"

Billy quickly did as he was told, walking around the garden, gathering handfuls of stones and depositing them into the tub.

Mrs Allen sat in her rocking chair, just outside of the garden windows, enjoying the shade.

He carried on for hours, but the longer he went, the harder rocks were to find, and the tub did not seem to be filling.

After a while, his arms were getting tired, and he wished to ask Mrs Allen if he could have a break. Before he'd even said a word, she'd barked, "What are you looking at me for, boy? Is the tub full yet?"

"No, Mrs Allen."

"Then you best get on with it!"

"But there aren't enough rocks. Please, I'm exhausted."

Her mouth twitched, and her lips pursed together.

She marched up to him, grabbed him by the ear, and dragged him back to the house, at which point she bent him over a chair.

He went to get up.

"Do not move," she said, her voice so quiet it was scary.

So he didn't move.

She returned a moment later with a ruler.

She pulled down his shorts. Held the ruler out. And smacked it hard against his backside.

It made him cry out.

But he didn't move. He wouldn't dare.

He knew that, if he did, the beatings would just get worse.

She struck him again. It felt like hot elastic being flicked against his skin.

She hit him again.

His buttocks were starting to swell.

She struck him again.

He sobbed, but he stifled it. He wanted to cry, but he refused to make a sound.

She struck him again.

He thought of Mummy.

Wondered what she'd be doing now.

It was a hot day. They'd probably be eating ice creams if he was still at home. They'd go for a walk in the park. The one where he met that friendly dog.

She struck him again.

Then she stepped back.

His bottom throbbed.

"Get up," she instructed. "And pull up your shorts, you look pathetic."

He did as he was told, then went back to the garden to collect rocks. Once Mrs Allen was satisfied that he had earned his dinner, she allowed him a small portion of soup with a slice of dry bread before he was sent to bed.

The next day, he was told to carry on filling the tub with rocks.

As he did, Mrs Allen stood at the kitchen window, watching him.

At no point did he ever question why.

WEEK TWO

CHAPTER ELEVEN

I'm struggling to tell what's a real memory and what's a dream. The two merge together like vodka into coke.

We sit as a family, watching the news, just as we did a week ago. This time Boris Johnson is not delivering the news conference. Our leader is in intensive care. It is a bunch of men who are experts in something, a foreign secretary and a scientist and someone to do with medicine. They go on and on and I barely hear a word.

I'm too focussed on last night.

Trying to decipher whether it was real.

"Our step-by-step action plan is aiming to slow the spread of the virus, so fewer people need to go to hospital at any one time, thereby protecting the NHS's capacity."

It happened at 2.00 a.m.

I know this because the first thing I saw when my eyes opened was the clock, and it was dead on the hour – not a minute sooner, and not a second later.

I was lying on my side. The room was cold but I was sweating.

And I sat up. Twisted until my feet met the carpet and I was sat upright, so straight it was like my back was fastened to a plank.

Then I stepped out of bed and walked to the bathroom.

And that's when I met the woman in the mirror.

"Of those who have contracted the virus, 1,408 have, very sadly, died. We express our dearest condolences to the families and friends of those who have passed away and I think those figures are a powerful reminder to us all of the importance of following the government's guidelines."

The woman in the mirror was old. Far older than I. She had grey, scraggly hair. Chaotic, curling in every direction. Her clothes were a light brown. Like the colour you'd find on curtains in a grandparent's house. Sickly and unappealing.

She looked incapable of happiness. Like her lips were unable to form the curve required to show pleasure. Her eyes were mad, her face was pale, her frown was intense.

Everything about her scared me.

"This is a united national effort and the spirit of selflessness shown by so many is an inspiration."

She said nothing, at first. Just looked at me. And I looked back. So sure it was a dream, but able to feel the weight in my legs like I wouldn't be able to if I weren't actually standing on them.

Was I imagining the weight on my legs?

Is it possible to dream feelings as well as actions?

"But many travellers haven't yet managed to get home. From young backpackers to retired couples on cruises. We appreciate the difficult predicament they find themselves in."

Then her mouth opened.

Her teeth were yellow. Her saliva black. Her nose curled up as she spoke, like a snarl.

Why haven't you been listening to me?

I... I don't know...

I have told you quite clearly, and yet you disobey me.

But I don't want to hurt my family.

But you are already hurting them.

No I'm not.

You hate them.

I don't hate them.

They think you hate them.

But I don't. Really, I don't. I love them. I'm just... A little bit lost right now.

"We also recognise the anxiety of families here in the UK, who are concerned to get their loved ones home. It is a worrying time for all of those who have been affected."

You won't touch your husband.

It's not that simple.

You shouldn't touch him.

What?

What he did was wrong, and he doesn't deserve your touch.

It's my kids I care about.

Oh, dearest Lisa, they are guilty too.

"We have a lot more to do, but we have already helped hundreds of thousands of Britons get home."

Drown them.

What?

The well.

No.

I'm not asking.

Please, don't make me do it.

I am not making you.

Yes, you are.

You will do so willingly.

What?

Because you hate them.

I love my children.

They are your husband's children. You can never fully love them.

But I do. Really, I do. I'd die for them.

But would you kill for them?

"We've not faced challenges in getting home from abroad, on this scale, in recent memory. Airports are closing down or preventing airlines from operating on a commercial basis."

Who are you?

Me?

Yes.

I'm your reflection.

You don't look like me.

What do you look like?

I'm young.

Are you?

Well, younger.

But you are angry.

I guess.

Resentful.

Okay, fine.

Full of hatred.

I don't know if–

So I am your reflection then.

"So, for those stranded, or for families nervously waiting for news and wanting to see their loved ones return home, we are doing everything we can."

Please, leave me alone.

You can leave at any time.

But you'll still be there. Won't you?

Always.

Then how can I get rid of you?

She didn't answer me. She just smiled. And I was wrong, she could smile – but, now I'd seen it, I decided that I preferred her grimace.

"We can all support our NHS by continuing to follow the guidance to stay at home, protect our NHS, and save lives."

The man on the news finishes.

I turn to Adam. He's on the other end of the sofa with our two children between us.

"Are you okay?" he asks.

For a fleeting moment, I entertain the thought of telling him no – no, I am not okay.

But it's not possible for a different person to appear in your reflection. It was in my head. And, considering what she was saying, that makes it all the scarier.

"What's wrong?" he says.

He can see it in the look on my face. My façade has dropped. I'm no longer hiding it.

So I return the mask and I smile.

"I'm fine," I tell him.

"Are you sure, because you–"

"I'm fine."

He hesitates. "I'm sure this is all going to be over soon."

"What?"

"The pandemic. What they are talking about. I'm sure it's only going to last a few months."

"Oh. That. Yes. Yes, I'm sure."

That is how disconnected we are, Adam. I'm distant and you think I'm worried about the world. That I'm scared by a virus.

But it's not what's happening outside our home that scares me, Adam.

It's these thoughts I keep having. These things I keep seeing, these dreams, these...

I open my mouth and I'm about to spill everything and tell him how I feel and that I need help and that I'm scared of myself, of him, of us, and then – then I don't.

I smile at him. He smiles back.

And that is what we're reduced to.

Fake smiles over the heads of our children.

And I start to wonder if we're ever going to be able to go back.

CHAPTER TWELVE

I want to know more about this house.

   I've been hesitant to admit it to myself, but being here gives me this odd sensation. Like the walls have eyes.

And now I've admitted it, I feel even more ridiculous.

I'm a rational person. I believe in what I can see. I understand that there are things we can't explain, but I don't go in for notions of religion that attempt to explain the inexplicable – I reserve my judgement until there is a basis for my opinion. I believe in evidence.

So that's what I want: evidence.

A reason why this house is starting to unsettle me. Some kind of explanation about why I keep feeling like I'm being watched. Like there's whispering behind my back.

And why on earth I would snap at my children.

As much as my marriage is falling apart, and I may seethe beneath the surface, I am never outwardly nasty. Even with Adam, I withhold my thoughts. And with my children... I would never do anything to upset them.

So why did I call my child an *inbred piece of shit*?

Just the thought makes me want to rush up to Tilly and

Jack, take them in my arms, squeeze them tight and keep apologising until I run out of breath.

I stand on a chair in the kitchen. The only place my phone gets the slightest bit of reception. I open Safari on my iPhone and search *Morosely Manor* on Google.

It takes a few minutes to load, and I scan the results. I see nothing right away; nothing that is directly about the house as such – but there is an article on World War 2 evacuees. Being in the country, I imagine this is the kind of area a lot of children were sent.

I add the keywords *List of Evacuees World War 2* to my search, and wonder if such records exist.

A number of PDFs come up. God knows how long it would take them to load with this connection, but they seem to be the most promising result – as they are of old documents. But I can't search the text in PDFs if all it contains are images of documents, meaning I'd have to sift through hundreds of pages to see if there's mention of this house.

I go back.

And then I do see something.

At the bottom of the searches. An article. Entitled *The Missing Evacuees of World War 2.* I open it and, as I do, I hear something. I look behind me and a pad of paper that was on the table is now on the floor. I think nothing of it, turn back to the article. After it finally loads, I read every word:

WITH THE MANY *tragedies of World War 2 – of which there were, of course, many – the number of missing evacuees is a concerning statistic that has never been fully explored. Maybe it has been overlooked because of the horrors of the time, or maybe it was a clerical error that was covered up – but there were many evacuees who never actually returned home.*

Of course, there could be numerous reasons. For example, their parents may have died, and they may not have had a home to return to. Alternatively, they may have found a happier home with their newfound carer.

However, there are some evacuees that never returned home and, when questions were asked by the mothers, there were few answers, if any.

Sometimes children would be taken from house to house, dropped off as and when they found someone to take them, and their teacher that dropped them off would make a record of it. Sometimes, however, those records were lost.

Of course, many of the children wrote home, and so shared with their parents where they were staying.

There was one woman, however, by the name of Caron James, whose son, William James – known as Billy to his family and friends – was evacuated after giving his mum a big hug and shedding a few tears, only to never be heard from again.

Out of curiosity, I did some research into Billy James. His teacher, Leonard Harding, died in a car crash when he was returning home from leaving evacuees with their hosts, and his records were lost in the blaze of the crash. I did, however, manage to track down the journals of Leonard Harding, and found some mention of the homes where he left some of the evacuees. Among them was Billy. Unfortunately, his mother died before I was able to tell her where he went.

According to Harding, Billy was left at a large, secluded house called Morosely Manor, with a spinster named Joan Hyacinth Allen. It is a house surrounded by fields with little life nearby, and only accessible by long, country roads.

Unfortunately, there are no records of Billy after that. Mrs Allen died during the war, left behind no relatives, and left no indication of what had happened to Billy after she passed away.

This is where the trail became cold, and I was unable to find anymore. I was desperate to know, if only through morbid curiosity, what happened to Billy James. How did he just disappear? Where did *he go? If he died during the war, why was his body not found? If he ran away, where did he end up? And why did he not send letters to his mother during the war, considering how much love there was between them?*

I guess we'll never know what happened to Billy.

As we won't with many of the children who disappeared once they were evacuated, never to be heard from again.

"Mum!"

I don't hear Tilly calling me. I stand on the kitchen chair in stunned silence, reading the last few paragraphs, over and over.

"Mum!"

How could a boy just disappear?

And this Mrs Allen woman... how did she die?

"Mum!" Tilly comes bursting into the kitchen, Jack behind her. "Jack hit me!"

"No I did not!" he protests. "We were playing tag and I tagged her."

"But he did it really hard!"

"I was just playing tag!"

I look at them. My mouth opens but I produce no words. My mind is on the article, not on their petty argument.

Then I remind myself that I'm a good mother. I listen to my children. I don't let things distract me. I return my phone to the top of the cupboard so we can use it as a hotspot and climb down from my chair.

"Perhaps," I say, "if you are unable to play tag nicely, you shouldn't play it at all."

"But I want to play it," says Tilly. "I just don't want him to tag me too hard."

"Sometimes he can't help it, Tilly. Sometimes Jack gets enthusiastic. You should love him for it."

"But Mum!"

"Where are your maths challenges? Have you finished them?"

"We were taking a break."

"Right, well break's over. Grab your iPads and carry on."

"But Mum, they are too difficult."

I was going to write a blog entry. I was going to vacuum upstairs. I was going to do some unpacking. But these children deserve my attention more.

"Then I will help you," I say. "Now go get them."

They run away and their stomps pound up the stairs, then they return moments later with their iPads. They sit at the table and load their maths challenges, being more patient with the slow connection than I am.

I do adore those children.

I really do.

Despite what the whispers on the wind say.

LISA'S LIFE LESSONS BLOG ENTRY 49: CHILDREN ARE OUR FUTURE

Children.

They make our lives complete, and they fill our days with noise.

We give them dreams while they take our sleep.

We teach them what we know, and they teach us the rest.

I will admit, I did find becoming a parent tough. I was nervous enough about having one child, and finding out I was having twins mortified me. It was a complicated birth, where they had to be delivered by caesarean. In fact, after they showed me my daughter, they weren't too sure whether they would bring my son out alive.

But he was alive, and I was blessed with two lives to love.

And I'd spent the last few months of pregnancy in brilliant maternity wear from *Polly's Pregnant Purchases*, such as these wonderful dungarees you can buy here (this is an affiliate link):

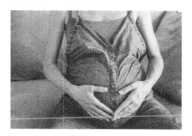

I enjoy watching them grow up, watching them learn about the world. We mustn't forget about the importance of mother-hood. About the brilliance of what we're doing. When we're tired, and we're breaking up another argument and we need to buy more food again and your husband is too busy working to give a shit – even when the voices scream at us to drown them and watch them gurgle until the last breath splutters out of their tiny bodies – we...

Well, we don't.

And I learnt all the parenting skills I have now through a selection of parenting books you can buy <u>here</u> from *Billy's Books* (this is an affiliate link):

No one ever told me it would be this tough.

No one ever said, hey, Lisa, here's a manual on what to do when this happens.

No one ever told me about the visions. The images I'd get. The invasive thoughts. The way the whispers on the wind insist and insist and insist that I

well
I
oh
what's
I… I forget what I was writing.

I will go over it later. I will redraft this post. I will do so after I've slept. I'll

Whats the

drown them
drown them
drown them
i don't understand
drown them
drown them
drown them
drown them
drown them
drown them

drown them
drown them
drown them

drown them
drown them
drown them

parenting is something we do becauseweretoldtodoit and i getmadsometimes and when i do someone has to pay and i just can't

Oh, and I almost forgot to mention, this knife is on sale at *Brendon's Butchery* here (this is an affiliate link):

I don't quite know what I've just written but she's telling me to post it.

So I will.

I must do what she says.

must do must do must do must do

I must *always* do what she says.

I'm beginning to understand that now.

Stay safe and stay well.

CHAPTER THIRTEEN

The children do their English assignments. A review of something they've watched or read. They sit at the table in silence. Tilly writes hers about her favourite book, *Matilda,* and she only loves the book because they share the same name. Jack does his on *The Avengers,* his favourite film, and I can see him struggling in the way he always does when he has to write something.

It's always astounded us how we can have two twins so dissimilar in abilities – Tilly, who is so bright I wouldn't be surprised if she turned out to be a genius, able to read from a young age, and always so observant, so astute – and then Jack, who can barely write at all, who rarely understands what's going on, who still calls me Mummy like he's three. I'm hoping his new school will cope with his difficulties far better than the last.

I turn back to my computer screen. I'm not too sure what I've written, but I don't proofread it. I'm not supposed to, I don't think. So I sign off my blog post, send it, and stare out the window with the end of a pen in my mouth. It's a nasty habit and I wish I didn't do it. My mother always used to knock it out of my mouth when she saw me doing it. My father didn't, though.

It's sunny outside. It's a shame the kids are inside doing work, but it's what they'd be doing if they were at school.

"Mum, how do you spell brilliant?"

I answer without looking at her.

"B. R. I. L. L. I. A. N. T."

I scratched my arm earlier. With my nails. I drew blood. I'm not sure why. It stung, but it was okay, like the pain was meant to be there. Like the pain was important. I was thinking of Adam. And I was thinking of…

I don't know what.

Having sex with him.

Hurting him, I think. Whilst having sex. Which is odd. It's not the kind of thing we've ever been into. I don't like being *fucked,* I like being *made love to.* And Adam knows it.

Perhaps that's why he went to his secretary. Perhaps she likes to be fucked, and that's what she could give him that I couldn't.

Or perhaps my body just doesn't do it for him anymore. I'm still thin, I guess. As thin as you can be after having kids. But it still doesn't look right.

"Mum, how do you spell writer? Does it start with an R?"

"No, it starts with a w. W. R. I. T. E. R."

A chopping board remains on the side from lunch. On it, the remnants of bread and cheese. Next to that, a knife.

I focus on the knife. Watch it intently. Like I could make it move of its own accord.

That's the one.

I get up and take the knife. Twirl it. Stare at the blade.

I see my reflection in it.

There are bags under my eyes. Heavy, grey ones. I look

older than I did yesterday. I suppose I am older than I was yesterday.

The country air is ageing me.

"Mum, how do you spell library?"

"L. I. B. R. A. R. Y."

I turn back to the knife. It's no longer in my hand.

It's not on the chopping board either.

I look on the floor. Search around me.

I haven't dropped it.

I have no idea where it's gone.

I get on my hands and knees. Search under the dishwasher. Stand up. Search the counter. The bowl.

It's nowhere.

Then I get back on my knees and... Well, I forget what I'm doing.

I'm searching for something, but cannot think what it is.

"Mum, how do you spell spectacular?"

"F. U. C. K. O. F. F. A. N. D. D. I. E."

"What? No it isn't. It doesn't start with an F."

I turn to look at her. A picture frame behind her falls suddenly to the side.

"What?"

"What's that, honey?"

"I said how do you spell spectacular?"

"Oh. Erm... S. P. E. C. T. A. C. U. L. A. R."

"See, no Fs."

"No what?"

She carries on with her writing.

And I carry on gazing out of the window.

In the distance, I can see the well. The sun shines on it, as if illuminating it in a holy glow. I stare at it until Tilly tells me she's done. Then she helps Jack finish his, though he doesn't understand half the words she tells him to use. Then I let them go play.

I read what they've written. Tilly's writing is wonderful. Lots of big words. A varied vocabulary. It's brilliant, really. Jack's is a lot more tedious. Shorter. Very few words with more than two syllables.

I delete it all and return to staring at the well.

CHAPTER FOURTEEN

It's 2.00 a.m. and my eyes shoot open and I'm awake again, though not fully.

I am never fully awake.

But my eyes are open and I'm aware, even if on a superficial level, that I must get out of bed.

So I sit up. Slide my legs from under the covers. Place my feet on the carpet. Feel the carpet between my toes. Stand.

Turn.

Walk.

And I'm in the bathroom.

And the woman in the mirror is there again.

She's beckoning me forward with her finger. Calling me to her like she has a treat.

I stand in the doorway and watch her. She's smiling today, but the smile is far more unsettling than her grimace. Her eyes are wide and her head keeps tilting and I feel like she's crazy.

But I also feel like she's right.

So I walk forward.

Lock the door.

I lock the door. We don't want Adam waking up.

Good girl. Now come here.

I approach her. Look at her.

The tap beneath the mirror provides a repetitive drip. Drip. Drip. Drip. Like a metronome that makes me fall deeper and deeper.

I take it you learnt about me.

I did.

You know that I died.

I do.

And Billy. What of him?

No one knows.

She cackles.

And Tilly. Jack. What of them?

I know what you're going to say.

If you know, then why is it not done?

I don't want to.

Yes, you do.

Okay, I do. But I shouldn't.

Yes, you should.

Adam wouldn't understand.

Then he should go too.

But why?

Do I need to give you an explanation, Lisa?

No. You don't.

Good girl. Now undress for me. I want to see you properly.

Yes, Mrs Allen.

I lift my vest over my head. I drop my pyjamas to the ground.

You're too thin. It's sickly. A girl your age should be plumper.

I'm sorry.

And what of that cellulite on your thighs? It's disgusting.

I'm sorry.

And those breasts. So peak and perky. You look like a little slut, and you deserve to be treated like one. Don't you?

Yes.

Your husband might covet this body, but it repulses me. You look like a child. Now put your clothes back on.

Yes, Mrs Allen.

I put my vest back on. My pyjamas.

You will use this body, Lisa.

Okay.

You will use it against him. Then you will kill him. Then the children...

I understand.

You will do as I tell you. You will not ignore me again.

Yes, Mrs Allen.

Now get out of my sight. You are sickening me.

I'm sorry.

I turn away. Unlock the door. Return to bed.

CHAPTER FIFTEEN

I wake up at 6.00 a.m. Adam is asleep next to me.

I place my hand on his chest. He smiles. Like he's having a nice dream. I run my hand down his torso until it reaches his waistband. He's sticky; he's been sweating during the night.

He opens his eyes. Looks at me. Goes to speak, but I put my hand over his mouth and shush him. I do not take that hand away.

He appears confused. Then my hand creeps under his waistband and grabs him and he understands. He finally understands.

He's already hard. I rub. Rough. Large movements. Fast.

He goes to object. Tries to tell me it's hurting him. I press my hand harder over his mouth, and now he can't speak at all. His voice is muffled.

He goes to move my hand, so I grab both of his hands and hold them behind his head and move over his body and mount him.

He struggles, but I am too strong. He doesn't understand how I'm so strong. Neither do I. But I am.

"Lisa, please, I don't–"

I shush him.

"Lisa, I don't like this, I think you should st–"

I hold his hands in place with one hand and use the other to grip his throat. I squeeze hard enough that he can no longer object, and his stupid voice stops and he can just splutter and I ride him, ride like a donkey, quickly, then quicker still, harder.

His eyes are wide.

He's staring up at me.

He looks scared. It makes me laugh.

He's struggling for breath. He's going red.

I ride him harder. He stiffens. He can't help but enjoy it even if he hates it.

"Li… sa…"

He manages to get words out so I squeeze harder.

"Pl… ease… st… op…"

I take my hand away. He gasps for air. He tries to speak so I slap him hard across the cheek.

I'm grinding him so hard now that it's hurting me. I am shoving him deeper and deeper inside of me and the friction is starting to burn.

"Lisa–"

Before he can object further, I reach under my pillow and I take the knife, and I hold it high above my head with both hands and I plunge it downwards and–

"Lisa, stop!"

And I stop.

Just before the tip of the blade reaches his chest.

His eyes are wide and vulnerable. Staring up at me.

He's inside of me. How is he inside of me?

Are we having sex?

He smacks the knife out of my hand and it goes flying across the room.

Why was I holding a knife?

He shoves me off of him, throwing me to the floor, and stands. Staring at me. Panting. Sweating. His mouth open. He is gobsmacked. Dumbfounded. Unable to comprehend what just happened.

What did just happen?

"What the fuck is wrong with you?"

What the fuck is wrong with me?

I try to remember what happened. I remember going to bed. I remember looking down at him with a knife in my hand.

But what happened in between?

"Lisa – seriously, I'm waiting to hear. What are you doing?"

I go to speak but I can't.

"And what the fuck is a knife doing under your pillow?"

What is a knife doing under my pillow?

"I… I don't know…"

"What do you mean you don't know? Is that the kind of sex you're into now? Choking me then stabbing me?"

"I… I don't…"

"Because there's this thing called consent, Lisa. You discuss these things first. And if we'd talked about it, I'd have been able to tell you what a fucking lunatic you are!"

"I… I don't know what just happened. How did a knife get there?"

"You know what, Lisa, I don't have time for this. You're full of shit, and I don't have time for it."

He grabs a pillow. A sheet from out of the cupboard.

"What are you doing?" I ask.

"I'm sleeping in the spare room from now on. You tell me when you want to be husband and wife again, then we can talk about me coming back in, but until then, I…"

He storms to the doorway. Pauses. Looks back at me.

"You could have killed me, Lisa," he says, and leaves.

He's right.

I could have.

What on earth came over me?

CHAPTER SIXTEEN

I daydream through the day. Maths in the morning. English in the afternoon. Playtime in the evening. Then tea. Then bed.

Adam and I watch television together once the kids are in bed. We sit at opposite ends of the sofa, and he doesn't say a word to me. I consider talking to him, but I'm not sure what to say. The silence has never mattered before, but it seems to matter now.

Maybe I should apologise.

I go to open my mouth, but he gets up and charges upstairs. I go to join him in bed.

When I do, he's in the spare room.

So I crawl into bed alone, wondering what's going on with me.

I can't understand what happened last night. What I did. Why I did it. What compelled me.

I had a knife in my hand, for Christ's sake. A knife! It was dangerous enough to have it in the bed, but I was holding it above me.

Maybe Adam drugged me.

But why would he?

And I was on top of him. That's hardly what you'd be doing if you'd been slipped rohypnol. As far as I'm aware, such victims are pretty out of it.

I can't find an explanation.

So I close my eyes, thinking I won't be able to sleep. But I do, and fairly quickly.

And I dream about the well.

I stand over it.

And stare.

The water is overflowing. It dribbles down the sides and moistens my bare feet. I'm wearing something, but I'm not wearing anything. It makes sense, in the way that dreams often do when presenting nonsense.

I want to feed the well.

I don't know what that means, but I want to.

I want to feed it until it chokes.

I reach my hand out. She places her hand on my wrist and guides it. It touches the water, resting on the surface, feeling how cold it is. It's so cold it hurts my palm.

But she holds my hand there.

And I let her.

And I stand.

And I stare.

The whole time, the whispers on the wind keep hissing in my ear…

And I listen to every word they say.

CHAPTER SEVENTEEN

When I awake in the morning, the space in the bed next to me feels bigger. Adam's normally up by the time I wake, so it's not unusual for me to wake up alone – but his side of the bed is cold. The duvet's still tucked down the side of the mattress. It's just so unused.

I look at the time. It's not seven yet. Perhaps he's still in bed.

I sit up. Twist. Place my feet on the carpet. My hand feels wet. I don't know if it's sweat, but the rest of me is dry.

I ignore it. Accept it. It doesn't matter. I push open the door, gently so the creak doesn't wake anyone, and I see the guest room door at the other end of the corridor. Closed. A little light beneath it. Adam must be up, but hasn't left the room yet.

I creep past the door to Tilly's room, then past Jack's room. Soon they will wake up and rush downstairs for children's morning television. So I speed up, and it occurs to me just how long this corridor is. There are plenty more closed doors I pass; rooms that will probably remain empty for a good while yet.

I reach Adam's room. I go to enter, then pause. I knock. It's strange that I'm knocking on the door to his room. Like I need permission to speak to my own husband.

He sighs loud enough for me to hear. There are a few stomps and the door opens, just a gap, revealing his disgruntled face and the bed hair I have come to know so well.

"What?" he grunts.

"Can I come in?" I whisper.

"Why?"

I look over my shoulder at Tilly and Jack's rooms. "Because I don't want to wake the kids."

He huffs. He thinks I'm using them to get in, doesn't he?

"Fine," he says, opens the door, and allows me in.

He's set up the room quite well. He has a side cabinet by the bed with a lamp and a clock and the latest book he's reading, some legal thriller, I think. His clothes are folded on a chair in the corner.

This doesn't look temporary; it looks like he's settled here.

"Wow," I say. "You've really made yourself at home."

He shakes his head and rolls his eyes. He takes some clothes and spreads them out on the bed. But he doesn't get changed yet. He doesn't want to get undressed in front of me.

"I don't know what's going on with me," I blurt out. "I'm sorry."

"I know what's going on with you," he says.

"You do?" I sound hopeful. He's being sarcastic.

"You don't want to break up our family, but you don't want to forgive me."

"No, that's not what I meant."

"It's all right, Lisa. I know I screwed up. But I just don't know when you're going to stop punishing me for it."

"I'm not–"

"I mean, for Christ's sake, a knife! In our bed! Never mind that you thought it would be exciting to threaten me with it during sex; what about the fact that we slept in that bed with the *knife*? That was so dangerous, Lisa."

"I know."

"So why did you do it?"

"I… er… well…" I stutter over syllables. "I don't know. I didn't know that I did."

"What?"

"I don't remember putting the knife there."

"So, what, you're saying the kids did it? I did it?"

"No, I know I did it. I just – don't remember doing it…"

"You're full of shit, Lisa. If you want to end this marriage, just say. I would rather that than all of this shit."

He grabs his clothes and storms into the ensuite. Locks the door. He pees, and doesn't bother trying to disguise the noise. He flushes. A minute or so later he re-enters the room in his clothes. Shirt and smart trousers. Even when he works from home, he's still dressed properly. I can't decide whether it's something I love about him, or something I hate.

"Make a decision, Lisa," he says. "Because if fucking around with me to make yourself feel better is going to cost me my life, I don't think it's worth it."

He marches to the door.

"That's not what I'm doing."

He stops.

"Then what are you doing?"

"I… I'm trying to forgive you."

"How?"

"What?"

"How are you trying to forgive me? What are you doing exactly?"

I don't have an answer. He steps toward me, covering me in his shadow, and jabs his finger in my direction.

"I messed up," he says. "I did. I've apologised. And I know it's unforgivable, but either you forgive it and we move on, or we don't. Because we can't continue in a marriage where you are resenting me all the time."

"I'm not–"

"Oh fuck off, Lisa, yes you are. I see it in your eyes. All the time. Every time I say something there's this tired glare. Every time I work a minute past five there's an eye roll. Every time I can't watch the kids you leer at me."

"I have to work too."

"You write a blog, Lisa! It brings in a few thousand a year! So who is it who's paying for this house, huh? Who is it? Because it sure as hell isn't you. And if I don't work, then we don't have a home. Simple as that."

"So I'm supposed to sacrifice everything for you?"

"No, you're just–" He stops. Pants. Realises he's losing his temper. Places a hand on his hip and a hand on his forehead. He's sweating.

"I didn't put the knife there to take revenge on you," I say. "I don't know why it's there. I feel like I'm losing control, and I need help. I feel like... Like this house... Like it's..."

"Now you're blaming the house?"

"No. Yes. I... I don't know."

He opens the door.

"You're full of crap, Lisa. And you need to decide whether you want this family or not."

He marches along the corridor and down the stairs.

Tilly is stood outside her room. In her pyjamas. Staring at me.

How much did she hear?

I wish it was Jack standing there. Jack wouldn't have a clue what was going on. But Tilly is too perceptive. She'll see this for what it is.

The dying love between her parents.

We're traumatising the poor child and she's not even a teenager yet.

I need to cry. I don't want her to see me. So I walk to my bedroom and shut the door.

No one disturbs me.

When I go downstairs an hour later, breakfast has already been eaten, Adam is in his office, and the kids are dressed and doing maths challenges on their iPad.

I don't know whether Adam organised the kids to be helpful – or to show that he can organise the kids far better than I can.

She tells me I know which it is.

She tells me he's poisoning me.

She tells me he deserves to die.

And, with the children working hard, I leave them to it and walk outside. To the end of the garden. To my well.

My sweet, sweet well.

I place my hand over it. Stare at it.

Yes, that's it.

Love it.

I do love it.

It's your well.

It is my well.

It's almost time, Lisa.

It is almost time.

And I am grateful to her for showing me that.

1939

CHAPTER EIGHTEEN

Considering there were only two of them living in Morosely Manor, Billy had an awful lot of dishes to wash. His back was aching from the vacuuming and his arms were aching from the sweeping, but he had been promised – this was his last chore. For the day, anyway. After this, he was free to do a pastime activity.

Pastime activities, however, were also restricted. He was either allowed to read the Bible – one of which Mrs Allen had so very kindly donated to him – or sit and listen to the radio. Both of which weren't particularly fun.

He missed his mum. Sometimes he'd lay awake at night, thinking of her, wondering what she was doing. He wished he could write to her, but Mrs Allen forbade it, claiming that his writing was childish and pathetic. She had said, "Some people are born to read and write, and some people are born to wash the dishes." It didn't take much to figure out which she thought he was.

Three booming knocks on the front door snapped him out of his thoughts. How peculiar. Who on earth could that be?

They'd never had a visitor before. He didn't think anyone even knew they were here.

He poked his head out of the kitchen. Mrs Allen was nowhere to be found.

Three booming knocks resounded throughout the house again.

"Mrs Allen?" Billy called.

Nothing. Just the empty echo of his voice.

He looked up the stairs. In the study. In the garden. He couldn't find her anywhere.

The three booming knocks echoed again.

He crept through the grand hallway, to the door, and said, "Who's there?"

"Giles Constance. Now open the door!"

Billy looked over his shoulder. What was he meant to do? Open it?

What if this man was here to help him? What if he was here to take Billy away from Mrs Allen?

He unbolted the door and went to turn the handle.

"What are you doing?"

Mrs Allen's voice made him jump. She was walking down the stairs. She didn't look happy.

"I – I couldn't find you," he said.

"So you thought you'd answer the door yourself?"

"Sorry, Mrs Allen."

"You will be. Now get out of the way."

Billy backed away. Mrs Allen raised her eyebrows and he backed away further, until he was in the kitchen and out of sight. Then he stopped. Pressed himself against the wall and peered around the doorway, listening intently.

Mrs Allen brushed herself down. Straightened her blouse. Had she combed her hair?

She opened the door. A man stood there. The same age as Mrs Allen, perhaps a little older. A large moustache and a hat in his hand and a grey suit and a grim, sneering expression, much like the one Mrs Allen wore all the time.

He did not look like a nice man.

"Mr Constance," Mrs Allen acknowledged. She was smiling at him, fiddling with a button on her blouse, the one just in front of her bosoms. Billy wondered if this man knew just how fake her smile was.

"Mrs Allen, I am here to speak to you about the Stevenson accounts."

"Oh, yes?"

"Mr Stevenson wishes to have his money back. It was in the remit of the will."

"Was it now?"

"And the house while we're at it."

"And is that what Mr Stevenson wants?"

"Yes, it is."

"And is that what you want?"

She stepped toward him. So close he could probably smell her breath. She was still fiddling with that button, still smiling, still looking up at him with this kind of... fake vulnerability.

This man might believe the tame look in her eyes, but Billy didn't. He wondered whether to warn the man, but he was a grown-up. Surely he'd know.

Besides, even if Billy wanted to warn him, he wouldn't dare; imagine what Mrs Allen would do to him if he did.

"But you are the lawyer, aren't you? You control what the papers say?"

"I do not know quite what you're suggesting."

"You know what I'm suggesting, Giles."

"Do I?"

"Yes, you do."

"Well, if you are suggesting what I think you are, I will do no such thing. And this conversation is over."

He turned to leave. She grabbed his arm.

"Seeing as you're here anyway…" she said.

"What is wrong with you? Are you hysterical, woman?"

"I am whatever you want me to be."

She stepped toward him. Placed her hand on his crotch. Rested it there. He looked at her, confused, but did not step away. She gently squeezed, and moved her mouth so close to his that their lips almost touched.

Billy gasped. Terrified that he was heard, he rushed back into the kitchen, and continued doing the dishes, pretending he saw nothing, and that he heard nothing. He wasn't quite sure what they were doing, but he knew it was bad, and he dreaded what Mrs Allen would do if she knew Billy was spying on her.

A few minutes later, Mrs Allen walked in and spoke to him. She did not wear the smile that she'd presented to the man.

"Go to your room," she said. "I will tell you when you can come out."

"Yes, Mrs Allen," he said, and scuttled past her. He noticed that the man was now standing in the hallway and his jacket and hat were hung up.

Billy rushed upstairs, into his bedroom, and shut the door behind him. The room contained nothing more than a bed and a Bible, but it wasn't the monotony that tortured him – it was the noises. Not long after he had shut that door, they started, muffled yet overwhelmingly loud. One *uh* after another. Mrs Allen's voice getting louder and louder until she was screaming.

Billy lay on the bed and pulled the pillow over his head, trying to drown it out.

* * *

JOAN REACHED BACK until her hands gripped his ankles. Her breasts pointed to the ceiling, and she knew he was looking at them.

This may be sinful, and she may not be young anymore – but she still had enough artificial charm and beauty about her to be able to manipulate a man as easily as making breakfast.

She shouted and grunted and screamed, getting louder and louder, making Giles think he was the best fuck in the world.

He smiled, thinking he was good enough to cause all this pleasure.

Then she leant forward, placing her hands on his wrists and holding them behind his head, grinding back and forth, looking deep into his eyes. They looked shocked, like he was surprised she could be sexual.

Like he had no idea she was just pretending.

She'd never married. And she'd never thrown her body around like some disgusting whore. But she knew a sin could be committed when it was for the greater good, and when she was willing to repent afterwards.

And *this* was for the greater good.

As he began to moan, as his climax was imminent, as he was reaching the point that he was unable to control the spasms of his body, she reached under the pillow, pulled out the knife, and stuck it into the side of his throat.

She felt his penis convulse and spew its juices inside of her as she dragged the blade across his throat.

She put her whole body behind it. Slitting a throat isn't as easy as one may think, and she had to use both arms to force the knife into his flesh, into his windpipe, and drag it across.

Blood sprayed over her face and she didn't blink.

By the time he was limp and her vagina was sticky with his semen, he was spluttering his final breaths.

She lifted herself off of him, stepped away, and watched him die.

Then looked down at herself.

She was disgusted.

Her naked flesh exposed to a man. His juices running down her leg. Oh, what a foul wench she appeared to be.

She went into the bathroom. Looked in the mirror. Saw her reflection looking back. Saw her disgusting, dirty breasts and her hard nipples and her sweaty flaps.

She turned the taps on and filled the bath. She soaked her body, washing the sin off her, and using the douche to ensure there was none of his vile seed left inside of her.

Then she pulled out the plug. Dried her body. And readied herself for what came next.

She needed to deal with the corpse, but it could wait. She needed to face the consequences of her actions first.

Her whip was in the bedside drawer. She took it out. Knelt. Held her breath. Tensed her muscles. Then slashed it across her back.

It stung like hell.

She looked over her shoulder. She could see a line of blood on the floor.

She slashed it again.

It hurt, but it wasn't enough.

So she stood.

Looked down at where she had allowed him to defile her. Where she had committed the most abhorrent of sin. Where only ungodly acts could occur.

And she slashed it.

And she cried out with anguish, and hated herself for doing so. She wasn't allowed to cry out. She was supposed to take her punishment as God would intend, and not be so impudent as to allow herself relief.

She decided that, as a result of her insolence, that slash didn't count.

So she did it again.

This time she bit her lip. Closed her eyes. Scrunched up her face. Held in any weeping. Any sound. Kept silent.

And slashed again.

She hit her thigh too, leaving red marks.

But it wasn't sufficient. Not yet. She hadn't repented anywhere near enough to be granted forgiveness for what she had just done.

Fornication outside of marriage was abominable. She had done it for good reason, which was why God might forgive her – but not until she had been duly punished. Not until she made it clear that she was willing to pay for her indiscretions.

So she slashed again. And again. Until the pain was so searing that she couldn't stand it anymore.

Then she did it again.

Then fell to her knees. Allowed herself tears. And looked up to Heaven and prayed for forgiveness.

Then she rolled the body up in the bedsheets and prepared it for disposal.

* * *

THE SILENCE WAS LOUDER than the screams, and it lasted a while.

Billy removed the pillow from his ears and listened, hoping to hear some sign of life. Where was this man now? Was he okay?

What had Mrs Allen done to him?

Maybe he'd left. Maybe she'd scared him away.

Maybe…

Mum would understand. She'd tell him how he was feeling. She'd explain what was happening.

He heard the quiet click of a door opening and closing at the other end of the corridor.

Billy abruptly sat up, on the edge of the bed, straightening his back.

Her steps grew louder then stopped outside his bedroom door. The doorknob turned, the door creaked open, and there she was. Her hair matted and crazy, her outfit grey and beige, the snarl returned to her face.

"Come with me," she instructed, and turned back to the corridor.

Billy did as he was told, trailing behind her until they reached her room. He paused in the doorway.

"What are you doing?" she snapped.

"You said I'm not to go in your room."

"Well, just this once, come in."

He stepped inside. The room smelt of sweat.

"See this?" she said, pointing to the bed.

On it was a big lump wrapped in a sheet. Thick red stains soaked through the tattered material.

What was it?

It was shaped like a human, but...

"I said, do you see it?" she repeated.

"Yes, Mrs Allen."

Was it *him*?

"You are to move it."

"Excuse me?"

"Are you deaf? I said you are to move it. Grab the end of the sheet and pull it off the bed."

"But I–"

"Do not answer me back, boy, or you will find yourself without supper."

Billy hadn't had any supper in two days. He'd had a small portion of bread for breakfast and for lunch, and he was starving. He didn't want to go another day without food.

And he didn't want to know what else she'd do to him if he didn't obey.

He took hold of the end of the sheet and pulled. It budged slightly. It was too heavy. He stopped, about to explain he couldn't do it, but he dare not, so he tried again.

"Come on, boy, put your back into it!"

He pulled again, scrunching up his face, moaning under the pressure, and managed to pull it off the bed and it landed on the floor.

From a crack in the sheets, he swore he could see an eye.

"Good, now follow me with it."

She proceeded out of the room and through the corridor.

Was he meant to pull it?

"Hurry up!"

He held the ends and pulled, but it wouldn't budge.

Mrs Allen stood at the top of the stairs, tapping her foot.

He heaved, his muscles throbbing, almost crying it was so heavy, but was unable to pull it.

"Oh for Pete's sake!"

Mrs Allen marched to his side, scowled at him, and took hold of another piece of the sheet, and they pulled it together.

They gradually moved it to the top of the stairs.

"Now we take it down the stairs."

Billy wiped sweat from his forehead. Panted. "It's too heavy, Mrs Allen."

"Oh, your mother must have been a wretched woman to create a child so rude!" Mrs Allen said. "A child who finds hard work so offensive. I would be so disappointed to have raised a child who was insolent as well as weak."

"But please, Mrs Allen, I…"

Her eyebrows narrowed. Rage flickered from cheek to cheek.

It struck terror in Billy's body, making him shiver, and he could feel his heart thudding faster and faster.

He would not disobey her. So, as requested, he dragged it with her to the first step, down the next, and down the next. It

113

wasn't as hard to get it down the steps as it was dragging it across the corridor, as its weight did most of the work. They just had to guide it.

Eventually, they brought it to the bottom of the stairs.

"Come on then," Mrs Allen said. "Nearly there."

By the time they'd dragged it through the kitchen and to the garden doors, Billy's knees were wobbling. His entire body felt like it needed to collapse.

But he had to do as he was told. He had to, or he'd starve. Or she'd hurt him again.

So they pulled it. An inch, then another inch, then another.

This continued across the back garden.

By the time they reached the well, Billy could barely stand.

"Now put it in the well," she said.

"In the well?"

"Are you deaf?"

Reluctantly, Billy put his arms beneath the sheet and tried to push it up. It was no good. It was too heavy. No matter how much he tried, he couldn't.

With a huff, Mrs Allen reluctantly put her hands under the sheet, as did Billy, and they lifted it, heaving with all their might.

Some may have seen this as mercy. Billy just knew it was because she wanted to hurry up and get this done.

They eventually pushed it over the side and, as it landed at the bottom of the well, the sheet fell halfway off, and a pair of eyes stared back up at him.

Billy didn't look. He didn't want to know.

Mrs Allen marched to the garden shed and opened the door. She pointed at the large tub of rocks Billy had almost filled.

"Come here," she said, and he walked up to her side. "I don't suppose you have the strength to pull this tub by yourself?"

He shook his head. His muscles ached so much he barely had the strength to stand.

"Well why don't you try?"

He walked to the other side of the tub and pushed. It didn't even budge.

"Push it over," she said.

"Sorry?"

"I said, push it over."

He'd spent weeks filling this tub, the last thing he wanted to do was push it over.

Mrs Allen, annoyed at his hesitance, walked to the other side of the tub and, together, they used all of their body strength to push it. The tub capsized, and rocks tumbled out.

"There is a wheelbarrow behind the shed. Go get it."

He retrieved the wheelbarrow and returned to Mrs Allen.

"You will take all of these rocks," she declared. "And you will throw them into the bottom of the well."

"But please, Mrs Allen, I'm really hungry."

She bent over and placed her face so close to his he could smell the garlic on her breath. "Well then I guess you better get on with it."

She added, "And hurry up," and began her walk back across the garden and into the house.

Billy knew he shouldn't have thrown whatever it was he threw into the well. He knew he shouldn't cover it in rocks. But he also knew that he was terrified.

If Mrs Allen was willing to hurt a stranger, what would she be willing to do to him?

He wanted to run away, but he had nowhere to go. He wanted to tell his mother, but Mrs Allen had taken his belongings and he didn't know her address, or how he would even go about posting a letter. And he wanted to tell someone what had happened, but there was no one to tell – and even if he did, they would not believe him.

His stomach rumbled.

He needed to eat.

So he put rocks in the wheelbarrow. Pushed it to the well. Then scooped up armfuls of rocks and threw them in.

They landed on

the sheet, but it would be a long while until he'd covered it completely.

In fact, it would take him well into the night.

Eventually, however, Billy covered the sheet with rubble, and whatever Mrs Allen had done was concealed.

It was almost 1.00a.m. when Billy was allowed some food – and even then, it was just a measly bowl of porridge.

WEEK THREE AND FOUR

CHAPTER NINETEEN

I t's a big house, and every day it seems to grow bigger.
And Tilly is scared of it.

Though she isn't sure why – aren't people supposed to be scared of monsters or clowns or spiders or heights? Not a house…

But she is scared. Because Mum is acting differently.

Dad would say she's just having a hard time right now. But Tilly knows better.

It's the house.

It's doing something to her.

Tilly doesn't know how she knows it, but she does.

Every day she watches Mum become a little stranger. It started with her leaning to the side, looking over her shoulder, like she's listening to someone next to her. She never says anything, but she always has this smile on her face, like someone's stroking her hair and she likes it.

Then there was the way she stared at the frog. If she mentioned it to Dad, he'd tell her she was imagining things – but he'd be wrong. She just had this… smile… like baddies have in the movies.

And then the muttering started. Just every now and then. To herself, or to someone else, or to no one at all. She'd be stood in the kitchen, and she'd just suddenly mutter something like, "no, I couldn't," or "yes, I know you do."

Sometimes people do this. Talk to themselves. Sometimes, when Jack's deep in thought, he starts acting out his thoughts. His eyes narrow, or he throws a punch, or he makes a noise like "Huzzah!"

But that's Jack. He's not all there, or so she overheard a teacher once saying. He was put in a group with the weird kids where they had to learn to read like she could when she was four. He is… different. Not quite with it.

Mum has always been *with it*.

Then there's the staring.

She stands in front of the mirror and just stares at it for ages. Tilly once walked into Mum's bedroom when she was supposed to be doing maths to tell Mum that Jack was using the iPad to go on games instead, and she found her. Staring. Gazing into her reflection, even talking to it.

And then there's the well.

She's obsessed with that well.

She just keeps going to check on it, like she used to check on Tilly and Jack. Tilly would be doing her work and Mum would check they were okay every half hour or so. Now she does that with the well instead.

Even when Mum's there, Tilly sees her staring out the window at it. Tilly would try and distract her by asking how to spell some of the big words she wanted to use, but Mum's gaze wouldn't shift.

It's just a well.

What's so special about it?

Tilly had been to look at it a few days ago, curious to see what was so special about it. She peered over the side, trying to see if there was something in there. All she found were pools of dirty water.

Then Mum came out and shouted.

"Get away from there!" she said.

Tilly leapt back.

She expected Mum to say, "it's not safe," or, "you might fall in."

Instead, she said, "That's *my* well. Not yours!"

Then Tilly ran away and Mum turned back to the well and stared at it for ages.

Tilly had watched her from the garden, waiting for her to snap again, to tell Tilly to go back in the house. But she didn't even notice Tilly was still there. Her stare was fixed on that well.

Then she came back in an hour or so later like nothing had happened.

And then there's the way she looks at Dad. It used to be with this glint in her eye, with this smile they would both share; like they were both in on this secret. But that smile isn't there anymore. Now she only looks at him with hatred. Like Dad's a disgusting little bug and Mum's looking forward to squishing him.

Tilly wants to go back to school.

She wants to see her friends.

She wants to go somewhere that isn't this house.

But there's nowhere to go. She'd walk for ages across the fields and find no one else. She would need Mum or Dad to drive her anywhere she'd want to go – but there is nowhere to go. The country is in lockdown, as Mum and Dad have explained. People are getting sick. They have to protect themselves from the sick people.

Only, Tilly is scared that her Mum is sick, and that Tilly is going to have to protect herself from her.

From Mum, who she loves so dearly.

She'd have to save her little brother too. Jack doesn't have a clue, and Dad is too busy with work; he doesn't seem to notice it either.

And now, as she sits with her family, watching the queen talk on television, she looks at Mum.

Mum watches the television, though it doesn't look like she's watching it, and Tilly wonders if Mum was still there at all.

CHAPTER TWENTY

"I am speaking to you at what I know is an increasingly challenging time. A time of disruption in the life of our country; a disruption that has brought grief to some, financial difficulties to many, and enormous changes to the daily lives of us all."

Tilly sits beside me. I feel her eyes on me.

I turn to her next to me. She and Jack are between me and Adam. And she's staring at me.

Smile at her.

I smile at her.

She's looking at me warily. Like something's wrong. Like I have something on my face.

Appease her.

"Are you okay, honey?" I ask her.

She nods vaguely. Turns away.

"I also want to thank those of you who are staying at home, thereby helping to protect the vulnerable, and sparing many families the pain already felt by those who have lost loved ones."

Queen Elizabeth II talks.

She's evil.

I don't listen.

I'm not interested.

She's a tyrant.

There are other rich, self-aggrandising, racist families we could listen to.

Let them watch.

I let them watch. If it helps them feel better.

It helps them feel connected to a world that's so far away.

The virus could have wiped out the whole world and the television is the only way we'd know about it.

I turn over my shoulder. I can see through the living room, through the kitchen, and out of the back doors.

It's still there.

The well is still there.

Are you taking care of it?

With all my heart, my dear friend. With all my heart.

"The attributes of self-discipline, of quiet good-humoured resolves and of fellow-feeling still characterise this country. The pride in who we are is not a part of our past, it defines our present and our future."

I reach my arm across the sofa. Place a hand on Adam's shoulder. He gives me a weak smile.

Does he know?

He'll never know.

Of course not.

Not until he dies.

Then he may realise in his final moments what he couldn't see all along.

And you will revel in the glory.

I will. Thank you, I will.

"And though self-isolating may at times be hard, many people of all faiths, and of none, are discovering that it presents an opportunity to slow down, pause and reflect, in prayer or meditation."

I check on the well again.

It's still there.

"Today, once again, many will feel a painful sense of separation from their loved ones. But now, as then, we know, deep down, that it is the right thing to do."

It is the right thing to do.

I love this house. It was the right choice. I'm at home here. I belong.

You belong to me.

I belong to you.

To this house.

My family will never leave.

"We will succeed – and that success will belong to every one of us."

I look up. Admire the wooden beams. The bumps in the ceiling. The bumps in the wall. It creates character. It creates a home.

And there is no one nearby to hear us.

We could scream until our lungs fall out and the only thing I will hear is the reassurance that *you are doing the right thing, my love.*

I am doing the right thing.

"We should take comfort that while we may have more still to endure, better days will return; we will meet again."

We will meet again.

You're right, Elizabeth.

We will.

I turn to Tilly. She's staring at me again. She looks unsettled.

Give her another smile.

I give her another smile.

Good girl.

She turns away. Looks to her father. Cuddles up to him. Holds Jack's hand.

"But for now, I send my thanks and warmest good wishes to you all."

And to you, my friend.

And to you.

LISA'S LIFE LESSONS BLOG ENTRY 50: WELL

the well is my friend the well is my friend the well is my friend
the well is my friend the well is my friend the well is my friend
the well is my friend the well is my friend the well is my friend
the well is my friend the well is my friend the well is my friend

and today we're discussing how best to boil your shoes

put the kettle on

there's <u>here</u> an affiliate thing:

and you get water to put in the kettle from the well the well

the well the well is my friend the well is my friend the well is
my friend the well is my friend the well is my friend

and once it comes to simmer you put them in, your shoes, put
them in, and wait until they are nice and ripe and

does one normally boil shoes?

here's <u>here</u> a link affiliate:

sometimes i wonder where this family came from why are
they here did i create them did i make them
she knows best

she always knows best

she does and you should listen to her

this is a wonderful wonderful house wonderful and it has a
well here and it going to be is very happy
thank you for following me on my blog on my new journey
into this well

this house

this home

i think things will work out very well the well is my friend the well is my friend the well is my friend the well is my friend the well is my friend the well is my friend the well is my friend.

here (affiliate):

take care of yourself please yes

its almost time

the pot boils
is anyone even listening?

how many undertakers does it take to move a family of four?

she knows best
she tells me what to do
and i

oh god

oh god she has me

she knows best she knows best she knows best she knows best
she knows best she knows best she knows best she knows best
she knows best she knows best she knows best she knows best
she knows best

please help me

she has me
and shes not letting go
and im afraid

i think im still in here somewhere

CHAPTER TWENTY-ONE

The woman in the reflection is always there.

Before, she would only be there when I woke up at night, when I'd step out of bed in the silence of sleep and talk to her.

Now she's always there.

When I walk past the bathroom, I glance inside and I see her. Sometimes when I stand at the window, watching the well, she's standing next to me, her hand on my back. I drink from a glass of water, and I see her eyes in the ripples of that water that contort the demented face that once mirrored my own.

I've found my fashion taste changing. No more jeans and vests and leggings and colourful bras. They are sinful. I now wear long skirts. Cardigans. Beige blouses.

I didn't know I had any, but I found a box. In the room. Behind the built-in wardrobe.

How did I get behind the built-in wardrobe?

You're a good girl, Lisa.

Thank you, Mrs Allen.

I'm proud of how far you've come.

Thank you, Mrs Allen.

Tilly walks past the bathroom door. She glances in and I shut the door.

Adam doesn't trust you.

Doesn't he?

Not since you didn't go through with my instructions.

I'm sorry, Mrs Allen.

You will not disobey me again.

I won't, Mrs Allen.

You will do it again – but not yet.

How do I get him to trust me again?

She considers this. Her thinking face looks like mine.

You need to make him feel comfortable again.

Yes, Mrs Allen.

You need to make an effort to work on our marriage.

Yes, Mrs Allen.

We need to make him think it's going well, that you're bonding, that you are making a considerable effort to improve our relationship.

I will, Mrs Allen.

We do not do anything else until I say.

I understand, Mrs Allen.

It is no good to pretend. We have to mean it. We have to show him we love him.

I do.

We have to show him.

We do.

We will show him.

Yes, we will.

She's proud of me. I'm doing well. After that hitch, we're back on track. I won't fail her again.

I leave the bathroom. Tilly stands across the corridor, staring at me.

"What's the matter?" I ask.

She doesn't say.

She turns and runs away. Like she's trying to play a game.

I don't have time for games. Not now.

I make my way to the office. I knock gently on the door. Push it open. Adam sits at his desk. Hand on his chin. Other hand on his mouse. Deep in thought.

I wait for the thought to pass.

"You okay?" he says.

He doesn't call me dear or honey. He's still angry.

"I thought, maybe, we could eat separately from the kids tonight," I say.

"How come?"

"Just as a treat. Maybe we could eat after they go to bed."

"Won't that be a little late?"

"It will only be half eight."

"Okay, then. What were you thinking?"

"It's a surprise."

He looks at me peculiarly. Curious. Oh, how excited I am to surprise him!

"I really want to try," I tell him. "I'm ready to forget now. And, if you'll let me, forgive. If you'll forgive me, that is."

"The knife is a pretty hard thing to–"

"I don't just mean the knife. I mean everything. Me accepting you back then hating you. It wasn't fair. If I wasn't willing to forgive, then I shouldn't have accepted you back. I've been a bad wife, and I'll do better."

He turns to me with the first genuine smile I've seen in a while. He's pleasantly surprised, I can tell. He's happy. This is what he's wanted.

That's good, Lisa. Well done. He's buying it.

"Are you sure?" he says. He's bound to be sceptical.

"Of course I'm sure. I love you so, so much."

He opens his arms. "I love you too. Come here."

I walk into his arms. Sit on his lap. Wrap my arms around his chest as he wraps his around me.

And he kisses me.

And it makes me want to vomit.

"I'll let you finish your work," I say. I stand. Walk to the door. Pause. Turn back to him. "I look forward to tonight. Let's make it special."

"I'd like that."

And I leave.

You did well.

So well.

I'm glad that you're proud of me.

All I want is for you to be proud of me.

CHAPTER TWENTY-TWO

I ask him to put the kids to bed, and he pulls a face like I've just made the most preposterous suggestion in the world. Even if I wasn't preparing us a wonderful dinner, I don't understand why he can't put them to bed every now and then.

No. Stop it. Stop being angry at him.

I need him to love me.

I need to love him.

So I find a dress. A black one. The first break from those baggy, formless clothes in a while, and I look in the mirror. She tells me it looks good. I think it does. It glides off the curves of my body, accentuating my figure and my breasts.

He won't be able to resist you – just remember to repent for your sins.

I will.

The main light in the dining room that adjoins the kitchen is bright and sterile. I turn it out. Find a few lamps from unpacked boxes and place them around the edges of the room. Then I put a dark red dining cloth over the table and place a few candles in the middle.

I find the posh china, which is still boxed, and unpack two

plates. I put the forks and knives beside them, perfectly symmetrical to one another. We have a bottle of red wine that I place between the candles, along with two glasses. By the time I'm done, the chicken korma I've prepared has finished cooking.

Chicken korma may not seem like the most romantic of meals – but it's his favourite. I used to make it for him all the time. So I make it again now, as an indication that I wish to return to those happy times.

I hear his steps. They are robotic and slow. He steps into the kitchen, wiping his eyes, and doesn't notice a single thing I've done.

"That was exhausting," he says. "They take ages to get to sleep."

He strolls past the table, turns on the big light, and gets a glass of water.

I turn off the big light and try not to be angry.

"Darling?" I say. "What do you think?"

He looks over his shoulder. That's when he notices the dress. And the candles. And the table.

"Did you do this?" he asks, and what a strange question – who on earth does he think did it?

"Yes," I say. "What do you think?"

"It looks great."

I can't tell if he means it.

"Well why don't you come sit down? You can pour the wine while I dish up."

He nods. Finishes his water, puts the glass in the sink, and joins me at the table. He walks like he's exhausted, but I can tell it's fake. It's like he wants me to admire him for reading our kids a story and putting them to bed. Something I've been doing every day for the past few years. I could point that out, but I know how that conversation would go – "You don't have to work like I do, do you? You just sit at home and write your blog. I have to go to court and work ten-hour days, on my feet."

Well, Adam, I don't just *sit at home* actually, I am usually on my feet trying to occupy the children and get the house nice for when you return home, and nor do I just *write my blog*, I spend time taking photos and researching and constructing a perfectly formed article. I have a life too, and it can be hard, and it doesn't revolve around you and your stupid court.

Calm down, my love.

Sorry.

These thoughts aren't helpful.

I know. You're right.

You need to love him. Admire him. Don't become passive aggressive.

I won't, Mrs Allen. I'll forget about it. I promise.

I serve the korma into two bowls and put one in Adam's place and one in mine. I take the naan bread out of the oven and take the rice out of the rice maker and place them on the table.

I sit opposite him and wait for him to say this looks nice. But he doesn't. He just dabs at the food and when he does finally speak, he says, "Does this have raisins in it?"

I smile. Raisins are my secret ingredient. It sounds like an odd choice for a korma, but it's actually quite a delectable addition.

"Yes."

"I'm allergic to raisins."

"What? You love raisins in korma."

"That was before I knew I was allergic."

He dabs at the sauce. He doesn't eat it. He pokes around the raisins, but there are too many, they are embedded in there.

"It's fine," he says. "I'll just have some naan bread and rice."

He pushes the korma away. He leaves the rice and rips off some naan bread.

Careful.

I know, Mrs Allen. I know.

"So how's work going?"

"Ah, it's really tough at the moment, you have no idea."

Because I'm just a measly wife who sits at home and writes her blog?

Stop it.

Sorry.

"How come?" I ask.

"We've got this case, this guy who says he's innocent but he's probably guilty."

"What did he do?"

"I can't tell you. Confidentiality and all that. Safe to say, though, he's not a nice man."

He rips off some more naan bread. I watch the uneaten korma. I began making the sauce this afternoon and left it in the slow cooker. That way, the sauce has time to infuse with the ingredients.

"Why don't you ask me a question?" I say, thinking how nice it would be if he asked me about my blog, or about my day, or about home-schooling, or about how I'm finding the new house.

"Are you going to be able to get up to make breakfast tomorrow? It was tough this morning."

I clench my teeth.

"Yep. Will do."

"Great."

I place some rice on the side of my plate. Scoop some up with a piece of chicken and some sauce. Eat it. It tastes good. Really good.

Then I stop eating. I huff. This isn't working.

I lean back.

"Do you want to do something else?" I ask.

"Like what?"

"I don't know. I did this so we could reconnect, and it doesn't seem to be working."

"I'm just tired."

"Can't you see I'm making an effort?"

"Yeah, I can. It's good. Well done."

"Well done?"

"It's just not that simple."

"Why not?"

"You kept a knife in our bed."

"Your secretary wanked you off."

"You endangered our life."

"You endangered our marriage."

"What, so we're even?"

"Not even close."

What did I tell you?

"Look," I say, "I just want to make it up to you. I want us to be okay."

"I know you do."

This isn't working. Try something else.

Fine.

I pick up my chair. Move it from opposite him to beside him. Take hold of his hand.

"Tell me about work," I say.

"I can't."

"Tell me what you can. Why is it stressing you out so much?"

"I just… There's a lot of expectation on me."

"Like what?"

He huffs. His eyes change. It seems to be working. He always loves talking about himself.

"We've got targets to reach, you know? I'm judged on

successful results in court – but surely I should be judged on the right verdict being reached, you know?"

"That must be tough."

"It is. When we're defending someone who's clearly guilty, it's not up to me to find a way for justice to prevail. There's just this expectation for me to find some legal loophole to get him off."

This is working.

"That doesn't seem fair."

You were right, Mrs Allen. Of course you were right.

"It doesn't. Sometimes I wonder if I chose the right vocation, you know? I mean, I'm good at it, and criminal defence is where the money is, but I often wonder whether I'd be better off doing another area of law. But then I've got you and the kids to think of, and this house, I need to keep doing it because we need the money."

This is why he wasn't talking. Why he wasn't responsive. Because he has all this negative energy. Because he's carrying around these feelings, these perplexing thoughts, and he needs to unload.

And his unloading means we're husband and wife again.

Once he's done, I take him up to bed. I take off my dress. Reveal the lacy lingerie.

I see him subtly check behind the pillow, but that's okay. He needs to learn to trust me again.

And we make love. Intensely. Staring into each other's eyes, like we used to. For the last few years he's spent the entire act of lovemaking with his eyes closed – but not now. Now, he wants to look at me.

When he's done, and he's asleep, I get out of bed. Mrs Allen shows me the whip she keeps in the drawer. I take it, and I lock myself in the bathroom, and I strip, and I kneel, and I repent for my sins, for the sin of how I dressed, for the sin of intercourse, and I do it on my back so no one will see it.

That's right. You committed sin because you had to – now you must ask His forgiveness.

I do, Mrs Allen.

Please, forgive me.

You are always such a good guide. Such a good teacher.

And I trust you to lead me. To tell me when it's time.

Soon, my dearest.

Soon, my love.

Soon.

CHAPTER TWENTY-THREE

Tilly's eyes open. It's morning. As she always does when she wakes up, she rolls to the side and looks at her clock. It's a special clock Mum bought her – it changes colour to amber when it's almost time to get up, then changes to green when she's allowed to go downstairs and watch cartoons.

Today, however, the alarm clock is off.

And Mum sits next to it.

"Mum?"

She smiles. But it isn't her smile.

"Hello, dear," she says. "I thought I'd come and wake you up this morning."

She reaches her arm out, placing it on Tilly's forehead, and strokes her hair out of her eyes.

"How are you feeling?"

"Okay."

A few months ago, Tilly was ill, and Mum woke her up and asked her the same thing with the same gesture. This is almost identical; from the way she sits, to the tone of her voice. Like she's mimicking a memory.

Only the smile is different.

"I'm making bacon and eggs for breakfast. Hurry down and you'll get some."

Those are the exact same words she'd used.

"Okay."

Mum tilts her head to the side and widens her smile. She places a gentle kiss on Tilly's forehead and leaves the room.

Tilly looks at her alarm clock.

She likes watching it turn to amber, then to green. It gives her time to wake up. Now, she has woken up quickly, and is already being ushered out of bed.

When she arrives downstairs, Dad is sat at the table with a coffee and a bacon sandwich. He smiles at her in the way he used to when Mum and Dad were happy and says, "Good morning."

Tilly smiles back.

Jack is also sat at the table, eating his bacon sandwich, wriggling around in his chair, chewing with his mouth open. She's said before how she doesn't like it when he chews with his mouth open, but Mum said that they had to make something called 'allowances' for Jack.

"Have a seat, darling," Mum says. She stands at the cooker, frying some bacon. "There's fresh orange juice or fresh apple juice or fresh pomegranate juice, help yourself."

Normally Tilly has a carton shoved in front of her. Now, however, she takes her favourite plastic cup, the one with Elsa from Frozen on it, and fills it with apple juice. Elsa looks back at her, grinning, wearing the same dress Tilly wore for Halloween last year.

"Would you like just bacon in your sandwich, or bacon and egg, just egg, or bacon with egg on the side?"

It takes Tilly a moment to think through all the options. "Just bacon, please."

"Coming up!"

Tilly looks at Dad. Doesn't he find Mum's behaviour weird?

He just drinks his coffee, scrolling through the news app on his iPad.

"So we have maths this morning," Mum says as she places a plate in front of Tilly, "then English this afternoon, followed by a bit of geography – then your father and I thought it would be nice if we went for an early evening stroll, the four of us – would you like that?"

Tilly nods. Bites into her sandwich. Keeps staring at Mum. They never do anything together. Either she goes somewhere with Dad, or she goes somewhere with Mum – never together. Not for a long time.

This should make her happy. Despite being so young, she knows that. She's smart. That's what all her teachers tell her. And she is perceptive, which means that she picks up on things.

It's not that she dislikes Mum being happy. She just seems too happy.

She keeps watching Mum as she eats her sandwich and Mum washes up. Jack's absorbed by his breakfast and Dad's engrossed in the news, but Tilly watches.

Mum stops washing a plate mid-stroke. She stares out the window. Gazing adoringly.

Tilly tries to figure out what she's staring at, and looks out the window over her shoulder. The only thing she can see is the well at the end of the garden.

She turns back to Mum. She looks so content, so loving, so completely mesmerised.

Then she mutters something to herself, so quietly that Tilly wouldn't notice if she wasn't watching, then she continues washing up.

She does this again a few more times, and Tilly watches carefully, trying to make out a few words.

But she can't.

And no one else seems to notice.

LISA'S LIFE LESSONS BLOG ENTRY 51: HOW TO SAVE A FAILING MARRIAGE

We've started to work on things.

She told me we should.

And I'm being a better wife. He's being a better husband.

We have to.

Otherwise he won't be compliant.

I do wifely duties and he works and I do wifely duties, despite this being 2020, despite this being an age where my career shouldn't be less important

sorry

i know im not supposed to do that

here's a picture <u>here</u> affiliate of a beautiful countryside:

To make a marriage work the first thing you need to do is
COMMUNICATE

and forgive all sins

if we confess our sins, he is faithful and just to forgive our sins
and to cleanse us from righteousness and here is a lovely whip
you can use to absolve those sins available in my bedroom
drawer <u>here</u>:

im doing what i must

i hope you understand that

is anybody there

i think i need help

im alone in this house

shes guiding me like a puppet

and i don't know how to make it stop

please make it stop stop stop stop stop stop stop stop stop stop
stop stop stop stop stop stop stop stop stop stop stop stop stop
stop stop stop stop stop stop stop stop stop stop stop stop stop

the house

its infested

she is in control

and i cant stop her

please help

im in here somewhere

im so scared shes going to kill my family

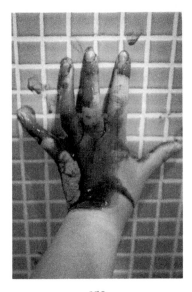

why is no one listening to me

she has me now

its only a matter of time

please tell my family I love them before they die

please dont pick apart my children to find out how they died

it was me

it was me

it was me

it was me

it was me

it was me

it was me

it was me

it was me

it was me

it was me
it was me
it was me
it was me
it was me
it was me

im so sorry

CHAPTER TWENTY-FOUR

It comes again at night. The voice. Waking me at 2.00 a.m.

The first thing I'm aware of is the rain. It's pounding against the window, thunder rumbling in the distance, and the house is creaking under the pressure.

But it's a strong house. It stands firm.

She entices me out of bed.

Get up, my dear.

I sit. Turn my body. Place my feet on the carpet. Stand. Walk to the bathroom.

The woman in the reflection tells me to go downstairs. To *check on where it will be done.*

So I do.

I step stoically across the hallway. Tilly's bedroom door is partly open. As is Jack's. I don't check on them. I continue down the stairs, my steps light to avoid the inevitable moan of ageing wood, and my bare feet carry me through the grand hallway, past the perfect architecture of a classic house, through the kitchen, and into the garden.

The rain is harsh and the droplets bombard me like bullets.

A few seconds and my pyjamas are soaked through. It doesn't bother me. Why should it?

I take the first step, then the other, my feet squelching on the wet soil. My ankles are muddy. Adam will notice. I will wipe them clean if I return.

That's it. Keep going. Learn the route. Make it familiar.

This is the route you took, wasn't it?

It is the route we take, my love.

It is the route we take.

My feet leave prints on the circle of bricks surrounding the well. I pause at its edge and peer in.

It's deep enough that one wouldn't be able to climb out, but shallow enough that it will flood. The water accumulates on top of the rubble. The rain has already filled it halfway. But this is good.

This is very good.

It's what I need.

The rain will not stop now.

It's sunny everywhere else.

It is.

But not here.

It will never stop raining here. Not until it's done.

Then it must be done.

I reach out my hand. Although I don't see her, I feel her behind me, reaching past my body and placing her hand on my arm. Her grip is firm and unrelenting, but her guidance is comforting. She stretches my arm toward the well, pushing it down until it touches the water's edge, and I have never felt more loved than I do right now.

Somehow, I just know. She will take care of me. She will show me the way. She will guide me.

Have I misled you at all so far?

Oh, no, not at all. If anything, you've been right about everything.

From beneath the water I see a face. I know it's not there, not now at least, but I know it was once. The man looks up at me. I can hear her laughing.

More than laughing.

Cackling. Hysterical cackling.

She enjoys this man's weak, weak eyes. The way he peers up at us in a way that says he'll never be able to leave.

And there's someone else in there.

Someone younger.

Much, much younger.

He stares up at me.

I place my arm in the water. Reach down.

He reaches his arm up.

He tries to talk to me.

Please stop, he says.

Please don't hurt your family, he says.

She's poisoning your thoughts, he says, she's controlling you, he says, get away from the house, he says, leave now and never come back or these walls will take your family and keep them forever, he says.

Don't listen to him.

But he seems sincere. He's young. Why is he so young?

He's insolent.

He's a child.

He's disobedient.

He's a child.

Do not be like Billy.

Billy?

"Mum?"

Before I can ask any more, a voice startles me.

The boy has left. He no longer looks up at me from the water. But she doesn't abandon me. She doesn't leave.

"Mum, what are you doing?"

Turn around. Look at your daughter.

156

I turn around and there's Tilly, standing there, coat over her pyjamas.

Tell her to come closer.

"Come over here, Tilly," I say.

My daughter does as I tell her.

CHAPTER TWENTY-FIVE

Tilly hears Mum's steps pass her room. Soft and silent. She looks at her clock. It's 2.00 a.m. What is she doing?

The rain launches itself at her bedroom window like a million rockets and it's too loud and she covers her ears and drowns it out.

What is Mum doing?

Even though she's not supposed to, even though she's forbidden from getting up before her clock turns green, she wants to know where Mum is going.

So she sits up. Turns. Places her feet on the carpet. Takes the few steps to the window and looks out.

Mum walks across the garden. Her movements are stiff, like a robot. Her feet are bare and her pyjamas are getting muddy. She walks to the well. Peers over it. Is she going to fall in?

Never mind what Tilly's allowed to do; she rushes out of her room.

She considers waking Dad, but he's rarely interested when Tilly comes to him with a problem. He normally responds with "Tell your mother, I'm busy." So she decides to go by herself.

She runs downstairs, stops by the coat hook, takes her padded raincoat, puts it on, then finds her shoes.

She picks up Mum's shoes, too. Maybe she'll want them.

She rushes to the backdoor. Opens it. Tries to see Mum through the rain, but her outline is barely discernible.

Tilly steps into the garden. The grass sinks beneath each step and she struggles to avoid puddles. She stops a few steps away from Mum, not wanting to approach.

Mum's talking to someone.

"He's a child," she says, then repeats it. "He's a child."

"Mum?" Tilly says.

She doesn't turn around straight away, but she does stop talking. Tilly stares at her back, her t-shirt soaked through, her hair drenched and dripping down her body. She must be so cold.

But she still doesn't turn around. Her head is tilted to the side, like she's listening carefully – but she's not listening to Tilly.

"Mum, what are you doing?"

She pauses, then she finally turns around. She has that smile again – the one that scares Tilly more than she's ever been scared by anything.

"Come over here, Tilly," she says.

She reaches her hand out.

Tilly wants to do what Mum says, she really does. She always does. She's not disobedient like Jack, or rude like Dad – she listens to Mum. Appreciates her.

But right now, at this very moment, the last thing she wants to do is approach Mum.

"Come on, it's okay," Mum says, waving toward herself with her outstretched hand.

The well is full of water. What is her obsession with that well?

"Why are you here, Mum?"

"Come here and I'll tell you."

Tilly doesn't want to, she really doesn't. But this is her Mum.

"I promise I won't hurt you," Mum reassures her.

Tilly takes a step forward. Pauses. Looks at the well, to Mum.

"Come on, it's okay."

Tilly steps forward and Mum's arm reaches her back. She guides her toward the well.

"Look in here," Mum says.

Tilly stands at the edge of the well. Looks inside.

Mum's hand on her back gets harder. More forceful. Making her lean over the well.

Tilly tries to get away from Mum's hand, but Mum grabs her coat in her fist and does not let her go. She pushes Tilly harder and harder over the well, until her whole body is pressed against it.

"Look inside," Mum says.

She keeps pushing Tilly forward, and for a moment, Tilly feels like she's about to fall in, then–

A boy's face looks at her. From in the water. A boy about her age. He whispers one clear, simple thing to her: "Run."

She heeds his warning, turns around, hits Mum's arms so they let go of her, and sprints across the garden, stumbling in the wet grass, back into the house, up the stairs, and into her room.

She takes off her coat and her shoes and gets into bed, and listens.

The rain responds.

Just rain.

Then the door to the garden shuts.

Seconds later, the first step creaks.

Gentle steps follow.

Up the stairs.

One by one.

Tilly grips her duvet. Pulls it over her. She's shivering.

The steps meet the hallway.

One step.

Another.

Toward Tilly's room.

They pause outside the door.

Tilly peers over the top of her duvet with wide eyes as the door creaks slightly open. Mum doesn't step inside; she just lingers at the doorway, her features only just decipherable in the darkness.

She smiles.

"Good night, dear," she says.

Tilly waits for more, but there isn't more.

"Good night, Mum."

Mum lingers a moment longer. Watching Tilly. Then she leaves.

The footsteps continue to her bedroom, and the door closes behind her.

Tilly barely sleeps for the rest of the night. She lays there, shaking, listening to the rain that does not stop.

1939

CHAPTER TWENTY-SIX

R ain hadn't hit Morosely Manor like this in a while. In
fact, Mrs Allen couldn't remember the last time
weather had attacked her home like this.

She grew up here.

She became a woman here.

It was her home, and no lawyer or brother or swindler was
going to take it from her. They would have to pry the keys
from her cold, dead hands, or suffer the consequences like
Giles Constance had.

She sat on the front porch, nudging her rocking chair back
and forth, slowly and rhythmically, giving a satisfying creak
with every movement.

Billy performed his chores in front of the house. She
watched him closely. He shoved the spade into the soil, dug up
a weed, placed it in the wheelbarrow. Dug up another weed,
placed it in the wheelbarrow. Over and over again, he made
this house even more beautiful.

"Mrs Allen?" he said, shouting to be heard across the rain.

She didn't respond.

He edged a little nearer.

"Mrs Allen?"

"My dearest," she said, "if you wish to talk to me, then you must come closer so I can hear you."

He dropped the spade, which irritated her, and he trudged toward her, his wellies heavy with mud.

"Mrs Allen?" he said as he reached the porch.

"Stay there," she said. She did not want his muddy footprints on the wooden beams of this delightful porch.

He stopped, squinting at her as rain poured from his scruffy hair and down his grubby face.

"What is it, my darling?" she asked.

"I'm a little thirsty," he said. "May I come in for a drink?"

"I assume you are not done yet?"

"No, Mrs Allen. I just want a drink."

"Very well. Just stand there a moment."

She looked him up and down. His coat was drenched, his trousers soaked, his wellies filthy. This certainly would not do.

"I do not wish for you get any mess in the house," she says. "If you would like to come in, then you need to strip first."

"But Mrs Allen–"

"I have made myself clear – my *darling*."

She smiled at him.

A really horrible smile.

He looked back at the wheelbarrow. At the work he'd been doing. Then back to her.

She raised her eyebrows, as if to indicate she was waiting.

He took his coat off and went to dump it on the porch.

"Ah, ah, ah!" Mrs Allen said. "Do not get mud on my porch. You can leave them where you are standing, and get dressed there once you're done."

She could see Billy's objections, almost voiced; but he did not dare to oppose her. He dumped his coat on the soggy grass.

"Good boy," she said.

He took off his wellies. Placed them neatly beside each other. Then took of his trousers and his t-shirt, leaving him in nothing but his white pants.

He went to step onto the porch.

"Excuse me," Mrs Allen said.

"What is it?"

"You are not quite done."

He looked down. "But Mrs Allen–"

"My darling, if you disobey me, I will be forced to hurt you."

He didn't argue. He took them off, and was finally allowed to step on the porch, shivering from the cold. It was the kind of weather his mother wouldn't let him stay out in for fear he was going to catch a cold.

But Mrs Allen wasn't his mother, and she quite deliberately made sure that was understood.

"Get a towel and dry your hair before you do anything else. I don't want it dripping on the floorboards."

"Yes, Mrs Allen."

He stepped inside the house, and Mrs Allen grinned.

Billy found a towel in the cupboard beneath the stairs. He wrapped it around his waist, giving himself some modesty, before taking another one and drying his hair.

The front door was still open. He could still see her silhouette, rocking slowly back and forth, every creak an omen of terror.

She'd killed that man.

She had.

Billy understood that now.

Would he be next?

That was why he had to do as he was told.

But what if he ran away? Surely, if he kept running, he would reach somewhere eventually? And they could take him back to Mum and he would be happy and she'd look after him and hug him and tell him everything would be okay.

He went into the kitchen. Took a glass. Filled it with water. Drank.

He couldn't stop his hands from shaking. He didn't feel well. He was going to get ill – that's what Mum used to say when he was wet, and she'd wrap a towel around him and hold him tight.

He washed the glass, not daring to leave a dirty glass out, and placed it in the cupboard. He caught sight of the knife block and turned away. Looked out of the kitchen window. Past the well were fields, lots of them. He could probably run faster than Mrs Allen. She was old. He wasn't. If he went now, he could do it.

He sneezed, took some kitchen roll and wiped his nose, then coughed again.

"Are you getting the flu?" came Mrs Allen's voice from behind him.

Her figure stood in the hallway. She didn't care for heating or light, so she was just an ominous figure in a dark room where he could see his breath in the air.

"No, Mrs Allen."

He coughed again. He tried not to, but he couldn't help it.

She took the towel from him and placed it in the washing machine.

"You're no good to me with a cold."

"I've not got a cold, Mrs Allen."

"If you're ill, what chores can you do then?"

"I'm fine, Mrs Allen."

"My dearest, I will determine if you are fine."

She placed her clammy palm on his forehead. She grimaced as she felt his temperature and shook her head.

Billy looked to the back door. He could make it into the back garden. He could.

"You're no good to me now."

She took a knife from the knife block.

Billy stared at the knife, thought of Mr Constance, and didn't hesitate – he ran to the back doors and tried to fling them open.

They were locked.

She paced toward him.

He twisted the lock and leapt into the garden. She swiped the knife at him, missed his neck, missed his back, but sunk the blade deep into his leg, and pulled it out again.

He howled as he fell to the floor.

But he wasn't going to wait to see what she did next.

He pushed himself up and tried to run further across the garden – but he couldn't. It was too hard. Every movement with his right leg was agony. Blood trickled down his naked skin, only to be washed away in the rain.

He heard her footsteps squelching the grass behind him.

He forced himself to limp as best as he could. He made it halfway across the garden before he fell and could not get up at all. The pain was hot and searing, and his leg had gone numb, and he couldn't feel his toes.

Moments later, Mrs Allen appeared above him. She took hold of his hair and dragged him across the muddy grass, covering his unblemished skin with dirt.

* * *

ENOUGH.

Enough enough enough.

Enough insolence.

Enough stupidity.

Enough self-entitlement and oh mummy I miss my mummy where's mummum *enough of it!*

It was DONE.

She could not stand his nonsense anymore.

She dragged him to the well. The water was overflowing. Pouring over the sides, splashing onto puddles on the surrounding bricks.

She placed him on the brick floor around the well, and he tried to get up again, so she smacked his face into the floor, cracking his nose, then smacked it again. His eyes opened and closed as he tried to stay conscious.

She held her hand out. Hovered it over the well. Felt it. The death. The decay of the man she'd left in here.

He was just muscle and bones now, which would go in time. No one was going to come out here. No one would think to look in the well.

"Please…" the boy said. "Please, Mrs Allen…"

Pathetic little urchin. His mother must be ashamed. A coward to the last.

She picked his head up by the hair, pulled him over the edge of the well, and held his face just above the water's surface.

"Please…" he whispered. "I'm sorry… I can do better…"

He won't do better.

And Mrs Allen did not care for his lies.

With a clump of his hair in her fist, she plunged his head under the water's surface and held it.

He struggled at first, but he was already weak; his mind was groggy and his fight was meek and his struggle was feeble.

It didn't last long, and within seconds he had stopped wriggling. He squirmed a little longer, but it was just reflex, nothing more; his pathetic little childish body reacting instinctively to a danger he was too stupid to perceive.

But his lack of movement didn't mean it was done yet. She wasn't a fool. He was probably only unconscious.

She kept his head under. His body twitched a little more, then stopped.

His chest stopped rising. But, even though he was no longer breathing, she kept holding him under.

And holding.

And holding.

Until the rain stopped, the sun came out, and she looked down at what she had done.

She took his legs, lifted them high, and placed him in the water. She gathered rocks and placed them on his chest and in his pockets until there was enough weight to carry him to the bottom of the well, and she watched him sink, sink lower, lower, until his body landed softly on the rubble, and she watched him, watched until the heat of the sun was too much and she needed to cool down inside.

She left Billy in his forever home at the bottom of the well, never to be heard of again.

WEEKS FIVE AND SIX

CHAPTER TWENTY-SEVEN

"Good afternoon, and welcome to the daily coronavirus press conference from Downing Street."

Huh?

What?

Where?

Tilly's looking at me.

Staring.

We gather on the sofa. Like we always do. Adam holds my hand. Like he never does. And we are a family.

A perfect, loving family.

Happy.

Content.

Faultless.

"Today's data shows that 327,608 people in the UK have now been tested for the coronavirus, 103,093 people have tested positive, and sadly, of those with the virus, 13,729 have now died."

"Oh, dear," Adam says. "How awful."

He holds his family a little tighter. Pulls me closer, along with Tilly and Jack.

Tilly is still looking at me.

"Based on this advice, the government has determined that current measures must remain in place for at least the next three weeks."

I don't think I can make it through three more weeks.

We don't need to, my dear.

Are you sure?

It's almost time. You're ready.

I feel ready.

But wait. What?

I don't want to…

Please don't make me…

Please, Billy, don't let her…

"I know that many people would like to hear more detail, some people are calling for exact dates, on what will happen next, and when. We are being as open as we responsibly can at this stage."

Adam holds me tighter.

This is love. It's what it feels like. I've missed it. We haven't had it in so long.

"I appreciate the impact of these measures is considerable on people and businesses across the country. The costs being shouldered. The sacrifices people are making. Being isolated from friends and family. Whole households, cooped up inside, all week long."

But the love. It's not real.

It's manipulated.

It's what it needs to be.

I really think I'm slipping. I'm falling, further and further.

And I will be the one to catch you.

"We get it. We know it's rough going at this time."

It's rough going?

"Every time I come to this lectern, and I read out the grim toll of people who have sadly passed away."

Huh?

"It makes me and it makes this government focus even harder on what we must do."

Please. I need help. Where's my help?

"And your efforts are paying off. There is light at the end of the tunnel."

You must go about your normal day.

"It's been an incredible national team effort."

You must act as you normally would.

"Let's stick together, let's see this through."

I will go about my normal day. I will act as I normally would.

"And let's defeat the coronavirus for good."

CHAPTER TWENTY-EIGHT

I go about my day as I normally would. I do all the things I usually do. I don't change my routine.

The rain still pours. The forecast says we'll have sun this week, but it doesn't reach Morosely Manor. The downpour is torrential, and the well is overflowing.

I find my dress from the box. I go in the shower.

I normally masturbate in the shower, so I masturbate again.

It doesn't work. I'm trying but it isn't working. It just hurts.

I rub harder, harder and harder, and I catch a nail but I keep going.

I think about Adam. I think about his cock. I think about riding him. I think about slitting his throat. I think about tearing his chest open and disembowelling him.

I rub harder.

I'm bleeding.

I'm rubbing so hard I'm bleeding.

But I mustn't stop. Not until I've finished.

I think more thoughts. Of Adam, of his body, his chest, his

beautiful face, his eyes, his throat cut open, his body laying open, my children watching.

The blood continues to trickle. It seeps between my fingers. Dribbles down my legs and mixes with water.

Blood is just thick water.

Why won't it stop bleeding?

I think of my kids and their hands as they clamber for me as they drown and they beg for me to stop and I tell them I love them and it's for the best and they go under and oh my God this is sinful and I'm bleeding I'm bleeding but I'm doing it and fuck oh fuck oh god I…

I lean my head against the tiles.

Let the water wash over me.

My fingers are raw. My clitoris stings. My legs feel sticky.

I wash the blood off with the shower head, dry myself off, and put on my outfit. Long, brown skirt and woolly cardigan.

I give the kids their work and tell Adam I'm off to the supermarket and to keep an eye on the kids. He's reluctant but we need to eat, so I go.

The queue to get in is long. I wait for ages and all the hand-wash is gone. I try to buy three tins of chopped tomatoes but I'm told I'm only allowed two so I buy a multipack instead.

I buy cleaning products. Sanitising wipes. Bin bags. A good fabric softener. Things I need to clean blood. I don't know why.

And I buy lots of food. Lots and lots of it. I know we're not going to eat it, but I also know I will not be leaving the house again. I don't know how, but I know that none of us will be. So, in that case, we need a lot of food, right?

Surely?

A feeling tells me we still won't need the food, but I buy it anyway.

I reach the checkout.

The woman asks me what I'm up to.

"Cooking my family," I say.

"Excuse me?"

"What?"

She's looking at me really oddly, then I realise my faux pas, and I CANNOT stop laughing.

"I – I – I mean cooking *for* my family," I say amongst the hysterics. She laughs nervously, then stares at me.

When I realise she's not laughing, I stop, and I hate her for being rude.

"Do you actually care what I'm up to today?"

"I was just making conv–"

"Ask me another disingenuous question again and I'll break your fucking neck."

She finishes putting my food through. Charges me money. I leave and she doesn't tell me to have a nice day.

I don't remember driving back, but I arrive at the house and close the door for what will be the last time.

Why will it be the last time?

I'm sorry, but I don't quite understand.

She doesn't answer. She's silent. Maybe she's sleeping. Maybe I just don't need to know.

Tilly is at the table, doing her maths.

Jack is on the floor of the living room, pushing his cars.

"Have you finished your maths?" I ask.

"No, I–"

"Then get back in there."

"But it's too hard."

"*Now.*"

He doesn't disobey me a second time. He returns and scrolls through the questions on his iPad.

"Will you help me, Mummy?"

I turn to him, incensed. Furious.

Before I can reply, Tilly is beside him.

"I'll help you," she says, and I leave them to it.

I finish unpacking, then go out to check on my well.
It's still there.
The water is overflowing.
And there are eyes looking up at me.
And I know what the well is for now.
And I know that I am almost ready.
I'll make her proud.

LISA'S LIFE LESSONS BLOG ENTRY 52: HOW TO MURDER YOUR FAMILY

this will be my last post

she has me and she will not let me go

i think this is the end

none of you have listened to me

none of you helped

shes coming

please shes coming

Hello, and welcome to today's blog post. Today we are discussing how best to murder your family.

Of course, there are many ways I could recommend. Many people have explored many options.

I know of some who have buried their lover underground, some who have stabbed them numerous times, and some who have enjoyed the slow death of asphyxiation, which allows one to look deep into their eyes as their life falls away and they slowly perish.

please help please help please help

Personally, I quite like the idea of performing the act with my hands. But, as a woman, often you have to be more inventive – we are unable to overpower a man with our muscles, nor are we able to push a knife far enough in to be sure that one stab wound would do it.

That is why I personally recommend a slit across the throat, from one side to the other, using both hands for maximum force.

shes going to hurt my family please shes going to make me and theres nothing i can do about it anymore

Of course, poison always works best, and is often the woman's weapon of choice – not just modern women, but through the ages

Personally, I like a good crucifixion.

why arent you listening to me

But, of course, sometimes you can't beat a good old-fashioned drowning.

shes infected me and she wont let me go now
not anymore

Stay safe and stay well.

please

please make it stop

im scared for my children

is anyone even out there anymore

is everyone sick

please

why wont you help

please use this as evidence that i tried to make it stop

that i tried to do something

i tried to communicate but no one was listening

so before you lock me up

or declare insanity

please know

i love my family i love my family i love my family i love my
family i love my family i love my family i love my family i love
my family i love my family i love my family i love my family i
love my family i love my family i love my family i love my
family i love my family

and i am so so scared for them

i have to go now

shes always watching

and i don't know how to fight her

close the curtains

block out the light

i never wanted this to happen

she made me

and i think its time for everyone to die now

CHAPTER TWENTY-NINE

K nock knock knock.
I stare at Tilly's bedroom door.

I know she's in there. I know she's behind it.

I can smell her.

She smells like filthy children. Like unwashed bedsheets and muddy baths.

"Tilly?"

My voice is melodic, a harmonious production of her name, a singsong of the word I gave her at birth. I do this to reassure her.

To let her know it's okay.

That it will be all right in the end.

That the pain won't last much longer.

"Tilly?"

There's shuffling. She moves.

Why is this door shut anyway?

Why is any door shut we are a family *a family* we should always love each other and take care of each other and this is precisely what I'm going to do:

I'm going to take care of you, Tilly.

"Tilly, come out. Listen to your mother."

Plods. Followed by the opening of the door. Followed by a petulant little face staring up at me.

We do not tolerate petulant children do we Mrs Allen *no we do not Lisa* oh we do not indeed.

"Come with me," I instruct.

"Where are we going?"

"I want to show you something."

"Is it the well?"

I stare at her. The sacrilegious little toad.

"I don't want to see the well, Mum."

"It is not *the* well. It is *my* well."

"It's raining outside."

"And it won't stop until you've seen the well."

It won't stop at all that's what Mrs Allen said *and I was right it will not stop* not until it's done *not until indeed* that's when the raining will stop *until then the well will overflow* which is just as we need it *exactly as we need it* exactly as we need it.

"Come with me, Tilly."

"I really don't want to, Mum."

"I am your mother and you will do as I say."

"Can I just carry on with my English? I was sitting on my bed, writing about–"

I grab her arm.

Children must learn. You do not disobey. You do not ignore. You do not protest. You do as you are told, and she will do as she is told, and I will not allow insolence in my house *insolence is worse than greed or lust or envy* or gluttony or wrath or sloth *or pride* or pride.

She wriggles. I grip harder. My fingers wrap around the tiny little bone, her tiny little muscle, and I drag her down the stairs, one by one, having to tolerate her struggle, her protests, and I would not dare suffer such disrespect. The audacity of it astounds me *oh how it astounds me too* it truly does astound me.

"Please, Mum."

I ignore her.

"Please, Mum, I don't want to see the well, I don't want to."

I turn. Hold her in place. Strike the palm of my hand across her cheek and the slap echoes.

"Do not answer me back, do not disobey me, and do not protest – you will do as I tell you."

Her hand rests on her cheek. Her eyes are full of hurt. She's wounded. She's shocked. She's upset. She can't understand how her loving mother just struck her in such a manner.

I can't understand how her loving mother just struck her in such a manner.

What am I doing *you are doing as you are told* but I just hit my child *she deserved it* but I never *she should have done as she was told.*

"Mum…" she gasps.

"You should have done as you were told," I tell her.

And I grab her dainty arm harder and drag her across the kitchen and she screams for her father but he's always too busy and we enter the garden.

The rain. It's hard against my skin. The pellets of water are getting stronger. The muddy lawn sinks and squelches. Just a few steps and my feet are covered in mud.

"Mum, it's raining!"

I turn around and she flinches.

That's all the warning she needs.

I pull her across the lawn and we reach the well and I shove her to the ground.

It's full. Overflowing. The water runs over the side.

I look into the water. A little boy looks back at me. Perhaps he and Tilly will be friends.

Perhaps they'll be happy together, down there.

"Come here," I tell Tilly.

She pulls herself out of my grasp, and I go to grab her

again, and she screams. Oh, how she screams. Her throat must be sore under the pressure, but it's pointless.

This house protects me. There's no one around. There's nothing she can do.

But before I can grab her arm again, she turns, and she runs. She slips on wet grass, but she pushes herself up again, and sprints back toward the house.

I look at the well.

I'm sorry *you will not fail me again Lisa* I will not *Tilly is too smart* not for us *maybe it's better you begin with another* maybe you're right.

Maybe she is right.

I walk back in. Knock on Tilly's door. I don't wait for an answer. I open it and place a mop and bucket before her.

"You got mud in the kitchen," I tell her.

It's filthy. Covered in tiny footprints.

"Clean it up."

She's resistant at first but my eyes show her that she should not be disobedient, and she does as I ask.

She takes the mop and bucket and cleans the floor. I sit at the table watching her.

She doesn't look up once.

CHAPTER THIRTY

The rule is: you do not disturb Dad when he's in his office unless it's an emergency.

The first thing he'd ask as soon as Tilly entered would be, "Have you asked your mum?"

But Tilly can't ask Mum.

She wants to. She wants to ask, why are you acting so strange? Why do you love that well so much? Why do you keep smiling like that?

Why do you want to hurt me?

But she can't.

So she approaches Dad's office. Slowly. Cautiously. The sound of computer keys tapping. The occasional huff. The ambient music in the background, something classical, played by an orchestra, mellow and relaxing.

Tilly takes a deep breath, tells herself this is an emergency, that she is okay to disturb him, then knocks on the door gently.

Too gently, in fact, as Dad doesn't seem to have heard her.

Another deep breath, and she knocks more firmly. A pause, then Dad responds.

"Come in."

She opens the door and waits in the doorway.

"Hang on," he says. He doesn't look away from the screen. He taps a few more keys, moves the mouse a bit, then finally looks at her.

"What's up?" he asks, short and snappy.

"I need to talk to you."

"Can Mum help? I'm busy."

She looks over her shoulder, worried that Mum may overhear her.

"I need to talk to you about Mum."

"Can it not wait, Tilly? I've got so much to do."

She goes to protest, then thinks better of it.

He evidently sees the disappointment on her face because, as she retreats, he says, "Okay, come in."

She steps inside, shyly, afraid to bother him, and shuts the door behind her.

"What's the matter?" he asks.

"It's Mum."

"What about her?"

"She's acting really strangely."

He looks down, deep in thought, then says, "Come here."

She walks over and he allows her to sit on his lap.

"I know Mum hasn't been herself for the last few weeks," he says. "Neither of us have. But it's okay. Mum and Dad were a little... upset... with each other for a while. But it's okay. We're figuring it out now."

"No, Dad, that's not it."

"Then what is it, darling?"

She hesitates. She has no idea how to say what she needs to say. In fact, she's not even sure what it is she needs to say.

"I don't know," she eventually concludes.

He smiles sympathetically. "Things are getting better now. I promise."

Reluctantly, she says, "Okay."

"We'll talk about it some more later, if you want to. Okay? For now, I really need to get this done."

"Okay."

"I love you."

"I love you too, Dad."

Her head drops as she meanders to the door.

Then he says, "Wait," and she stops and turns back to him.

"What's that?" he asks.

"What's what?"

He points to her arm. "That."

She looks at her arm. There are bruises where Mum had been grabbing her earlier. Two next to each other, one in the shape of Mum's thumb, and one in the shape of her fingers.

She goes to answer, but doesn't know what to say.

Dad finally leaves his seat, walks toward her, and kneels down. He takes her arm and looks at it.

"This looks like someone's been grabbing you," he says. "Was it Jack?"

Tilly shakes her head. Dad inspects it more closely.

"It's too big for Jack. Was this..."

He looks Tilly in the eyes. Suddenly, his face is awash with sympathy

"Did Mum do this?" he asks.

She hesitates. Then nods.

"Is this what you were trying to tell me?"

It wasn't exactly what she was trying to tell him; it wasn't the whole story. But it was a large portion of it, so she nods again.

"Gosh," he says. "I'm so sorry I wasn't listening to you, Tilly. How did she do this?"

"She grabbed me earlier."

"Why did she do that?"

Tilly shrugs. "She wanted to show me the well."

"The well?" He looks confused. He really doesn't know what's going on, does he? "Why did she want to show you the well?"

"I don't know, Dad. She really likes the well."

He looks confused. She doesn't know how else to say it.

"Where's Mum now?"

"Downstairs, I think. Looking in the mirror. She's always looking in the mirror."

"Okay. Well why don't you get your iPad and you can do your work in here this afternoon, yeah?"

"Okay."

She nods and rushes away, returning a few minutes later with her iPad, her hoody, and her beanbag chair. Everything she needs to settle in for the afternoon.

At first, she's relieved. Dad knows. He will keep her safe.

Then she thinks… but what about tomorrow?

Or the day after that?

And the day after that?

How will Dad protect her when he has no idea Mum is crazy?

Jack is clueless. Dad is clueless.

She realises that there may not be anyone to help her.

And she has never felt more alone.

CHAPTER THIRTY-ONE

D arkness meets the garden. The trees cast shadows, the puddles glisten in moonlight, the leaves fight the wind – and the rain destroys it all.

But it doesn't destroy the well.

They think they are safe inside.

They think they are safe with me.

Adam walks into the bedroom. He looks at me. I can feel his eyes burning my back. I don't turn away from the window; I'm enjoying the sight.

Soon, I won't be able to enjoy it any longer. She says to relish it while I can. And I'm glad we came here. Grateful I could experience life amongst nothingness. Pleased to have witnessed the tranquillity of emptiness, the hopefulness of silence. It's been peaceful. And the house accepted me as its own. And I am grateful.

I am always grateful to you for what you've taught me.

"Are you coming to bed?" Adam asks.

He's angry about something. He has that voice. The one I thought I'd destroyed. Our marriage is happy again, why is he ruining that?

"Lisa?"

I turn around. Flickers of lightning illuminate his face. I miss the sight of the rain.

"I said are you coming to bed?"

He waits for an answer. I don't give one. He huffs and pulls back the covers for himself.

"What's the matter?" I ask.

He pauses. Sighs.

"What happened with Tilly this afternoon?" he says. He doesn't look at me.

"With Tilly?"

"Yes. Our daughter. Tilly. What happened?"

"I don't know what happened. Is she okay?"

Now he looks at me.

"The mark on her arm."

"What mark?"

He keeps making and unmaking his side of the bed. He doesn't stop moving. He looks back at me then turns away.

"The bruise. The one you gave her. Where you'd grabbed her."

"I was moving her."

"Why?"

"Because she wasn't moving."

"And why were you trying to move her?"

"Because she was resisting."

He stops making and unmaking his side of the bed and turns to me. He approaches me, hands on his hips, shaking his head.

"Why was she resisting, Lisa?"

I don't answer him. I don't know why she was resisting. I was only trying to show her my well.

"Tilly is a smart girl," he says. "She's not Jack. She's pretty switched on, and she's not a trouble child. If she was refusing to go somewhere or do something, I'd imagine there'd be a pretty good reason."

I shrug. "I don't know what to tell you, Adam."

"For fuck's sake, Lisa!" He throws his arms in the air, turns away from me, then turns back. It's ever so dramatic. "I don't know what to say to you anymore. The way you're looking at me now, the way you're standing there, it – can I be honest with you, Lisa?"

Why wouldn't you be?

"Yes."

He steps toward me. Takes my hands in his. Peers deep into my eyes like he's trying to find my soul.

He won't find it there. You've hidden it.

"I'm scared."

"Scared?"

"Of you. There's something off about you. I don't know what it is, I can't quite put my finger on it. Don't get me wrong, I'm glad we're finally connecting again, but... I don't know. Maybe moving out here wasn't the best idea."

He keeps talking. So much talking. Does he ever stop?

I wonder what it would be like to kill him right now. You tell me to wait until he can't fight back. That he'd be too strong for me. I listen.

"Maybe we should leave this house for a bit," he suggests. "I don't know, get away. Take the kids somewhere."

I won't let him take me away from here.

I won't let him take me away from you.

"What do you think?"

"Where would we go? The whole country's on lockdown."

"I don't know. I'm sure there is some Airbnb somewhere that's still operating."

"It's not allowed, Adam. We have to stay at home. For the good of the country."

"Maybe we should just move then. Back to London."

"All house moves have been delayed, Adam. We have to stay at home. For the good of the country."

"Lisa, can you hear yourself?"

"We have to stay here."

"We're trapped here."

"There's plenty of fields to walk in."

"Aside from the supermarket, you haven't seen anyone else in weeks. Neither have I. Or the kids. I never thought, when we chose to come here, that we'd be stuck here, not able to go anywhere or see anyone."

"Everything we want is here, Adam."

"I don't care about lockdown. I don't care about the virus. When it comes to your sanity, and protecting our kids, *that* comes first, and if that means leaving, then…"

I place a hand on his cheek. He closes his eyes. It appeases him. Calms him. Oh, how pathetic men are.

"We don't need to run away from anything, my dearest," I tell him.

"But I'm worried about you."

"So long as you love me, I have all I need."

"But the kids…"

"They are fine. I'm sorry for what I did today. I must have grabbed too hard. I would never hurt my children, surely you know that?"

He nods. Looks guilty for thinking it.

"Things have been tough," I say. "But they are getting better. I know they are. I will talk to Tilly tomorrow, tell her I'm sorry, make sure she's okay."

"You promise?"

"Of course. I would never hurt my children."

"I know…"

"Things have been tough. But they are getting better."

"You sure?"

"Yes. And I would never hurt my children. Surely…"

He looks at me peculiarly.

"What?" I ask.

"You just seem so different."

I lean my forehead against his. "I'm still the same. And I still love you."

He tells me he loves me.

He kisses me.

We climb into bed. He puts his arm around me. I don't even bother sleeping. I lie there and wait until 2.00 a.m.

Until the hour arrives.

Until I get to speak to you.

CHAPTER THIRTY-TWO

Your attempts have been feeble.
    I'm sorry.
You shouldn't have let her get away from the well.
I'm sorry.
You shouldn't have failed to kill Adam before.
I'm sorry.
I will not tolerate this again.
I know.
It's time.
You've said that before.
Now I mean it.
I understand.
Tomorrow evening – it ends, one way or the other.
But I'm scared.
Don't be so pathetic.
What if I can't?
You won't.
What do you mean?
You will be a puppet.
A puppet?

My puppet.

I don't understand.

I will guide you every step of the way.

You will?

My hands will rest on your arms, you will feel me near, and I will guide you.

Thank you.

Together, we will do it.

Thank you, so, so much.

Together, we will do it as it was done before.

You are so good to me.

Together, we will save your family from a lifetime of pain.

You are so good to us.

Then we can be together forever.

Here?

Of course.

Thank you, Mrs Allen.

You are welcome my dear.

I love you.

I know. Now go back to sleep.

Yes, Mrs Allen.

Always, Mrs Allen.

I will let you guide me, Mrs Allen.

And finally this will be over.

And we will be at peace.

CHAPTER THIRTY-THREE

The glory of sun emerged from between the clouds. Light glistened in the puddles. Shadows formed over the well. Mrs Allen was on her knees. Staring down the well. Peering into the gaping hole. All the water was gone and there was just an empty face. Pale skin. He didn't move.

Did she do this?

This boy had a mother.

She couldn't remember why she'd done it. She's been so mad, so enraged. He'd done something to deserve it, she was sure.

But now, she couldn't think of a single thing the child had done wrong.

She could get help, but it would be pointless. There was a war on. By the time someone was willing to come out here, his body would already be rotting. His stink would infest the well, and there would be no way to get away from what she'd done.

What she'd done.

She'd done this.

What she'd...

Her eyes scrunched up. She cried, but no tears came out,

no matter how much she forced them. Something had taken her over, some kind of wrath had gripped her, and it only let her go now, once she had done what it wished her to do.

She had taken the life of a boy who depended on her to live.

She'd fed him. Given him clothes. Given him chores. She'd done everything she was taught one was supposed to do for a child.

Then she'd taken it away from him.

Her head lifted. Struck with a sudden thought. The body...

More people would be round. Her brother wanted the house. He was determined to evict her from it. Once he realised his lawyer wouldn't return, he'd just send another one. And another one, and another one, and another one...

And she could not let any of them know what she'd done.

She could not handle the shame.

She stood. Looked for a solution.

She could bury him. The soil was soft from the incessant rain, it would take effort to get him out of the well, but if she could she might be able to dig a hole and bury him. She could dig a deep hole, one far too deep for anyone to find, not in her lifetime anyway.

But she could not find the energy to dig as much as she needed.

She could burn his body. Set fire to it until he was just bones, then grind those bones up until they were dust, then give them to the wind.

But it would take a fire with an intense rage to turn this child to ash.

She could leave him to the well.

Her precious well.

Yes. She would give him to it, and the well would protect her. It was part of this house, and Morosely Manor had always treated her well.

He could decompose in there. Become bone. Leave his skin to rot.

He would be happy in there. Still. Peaceful.

He belonged to the house now.

Morosely Manor had guided her. Had told her how a child should act, and how to deal with Giles Constance. They belonged to the house now, just as she did.

She'd done well.

She'd demonstrated her love. Her obedience.

But the house was not done.

She turned back to its looming presence. It called for her. Told her there was one more deed she needed to do. One more task it wished of her. One more thing it wished to have.

"My life," she whispered.

She did not question the house.

She removed her shoes and placed one foot after another across the sinking soil, feeling each squelch whilst feeling nothing at all.

She made it into the house and removed her cardigan.

The house would want her exposed. It would want her form. God would want her honesty and her dignity and if that's what He wanted, if that's what *the house* wanted, then that was what she would give to it.

So she unbuttoned her blouse. Placed it on the table. Unhooked the belt of her skirt and placed it beside it. Removed her girdle. Her brassiere. Her bloomers.

She took rope from the closet and walked up the stairs, wet prints trailing her foreboding ascent.

It called to her. It beckoned her. Morosely Manor wanted her and, like any subservient mistress, she obeyed what her true love wished without question.

She entered her bedroom. Looked up to the wooden beams. Took the chair by her dresser and stood on it, using the height to hook the rope around the beam and create a noose.

She tugged it. Checked its strength. It would not yield. The beam would retain its strength. The rope would grant no pity.

She tied the noose around her neck, closed her eyes, and kicked the chair away.

Her neck did not snap. It was not quick. Instead, she forced herself to hang there, unable to breathe, snapping for air. She did not wish for oxygen but her body's instinct was to try, and it tried without relenting.

Her thoughts did not heed regret, nor did they entertain misery. They simply reminded her of her love for one to whom she gave her life so willingly.

She'd said goodbye to her parents here, and she'd done it just as the house wished her to do.

The man she was once meant to marry was given to the house in accordance to its wishes.

And now it was she, along with Billy and Giles, who would be given.

And, despite her death, they would not be her final sacrifice.

She did not do these things out of hatred or pain, oh no – her actions were out of love, the purest known to mankind; an epic love for the only entity that she had ever truly been in love with.

And when the suffocating ceased, and the dying ended, and she was just a corpse rocking back and forth, she was finally content enough to open her eyes, let herself down, and submerge herself into the walls, into the floor, into the air, into *the mirror.*

She wasn't Morosely's lover anymore; she *was* Morosely.

And they would forever be united as one.

THE FINAL WEEK

CHAPTER THIRTY-FOUR

The keyboard taps behind the door and he works so hard but there is one thing, and one thing only, that men cannot resist.

I open the door. He looks at me. He says nothing. He sees what I'm wearing and what I'm offering and I can see those words almost protruding from his mouth: I need to do work.

I stride forward and press a finger against his lips. His facial expression doesn't change. He still needs to do stuff. But he'll change his mind.

I go to my knees. He can see down the cleavage of this negligee. He wants to ask "what about the kids" but the kids are busy. I left Tilly in charge. She's stricter than either of us. She and Jack will be working for hours.

I undo his belt.

"Really, Lisa, I can't, I have to–"

I take him in my mouth and he shuts up.

Then I release him and just hold it, loosely, my finger and thumb around the base.

I lick it and I say, "I can stop if you want me to."

But he doesn't want me to.

Fuck work.

He doesn't say anything, but the hand on the back of my head pushing me tells me what I need to know.

I lick around the edge of the foreskin. Run my tongue over the shaft. Look up at him, look him dead in the eyes as I take it in my mouth and move my head back and forth. He hardens and he stiffens and this is exactly how I want him *exactly how we want him my love* exactly how we want him.

I let her take control and she tells me when to go faster, and she tells me when to stop, just as I feel him tense and I feel him harden even more.

"Oh, no, don't stop there."

But I don't want him to. Not yet.

So I stand.

I tell him, "If you want to carry on, you're going to have to come with me to the bedroom."

There are no protests about work, not even a mention about what he has to do, and he holds his trousers around his waist and checks the coast is clear *lead him* I lead him into the bedroom *place him on the bed* and I place him on the bed and I mount him.

"Take it off," he tells me.

I obey his request and remove the negligee and suck in my breath and let him see those perky little breasts that he used to love so much.

I don't tell him to remove his clothes. His underwear around his ankles is just fine. He looks pathetic and helpless and I place him inside of me and I stretch my body as I grind him and he stares at me, amazed, like he's never seen this body before, like it's something new, like it's better than remembered.

He doesn't hold himself off and he doesn't want to see if I'm close, he just starts moaning, starts saying oh yeah, oh

God, oh keep going *and we have him just where we want him* he is just where we want him.

And I feel him expand and explode.

And I place my hands either side of his pillow, watch his face as it morphs into powerlessness, and I shove my lips against his mouth as he finishes with such force he yelps and I reach under the pillow *grab it* and I grab the knife *take it* and I take the knife *slit it* and he's still moaning and he's just finishing *now Lisa* and I hold the knife out to the side *hurry up* and this time I do not fail.

This time. I. Do. Not. Fail.

Good girl, Lisa. Very good girl.

He can't scream as the knife has penetrated too deep into his throat and I feel her hand around mine, guiding it.

I draw the knife across his neck, dragging it, and I know I don't have the strength to do this bit on my own but with two women's effort behind it I can and I pull it and drag it across until the front of his neck is a long, gaping wound.

Then I shove the knife back into his neck and do it all over again, hacking at it like I'm sawing wood, cutting into it, and the arteries are torn and squirting over the walls and it's so deep the thyroid cartilage has been penetrated and he's still gagging and spluttering but not for much longer.

Not for much longer.

I lean up. He's still inside of me. Limp. Sticky. But I don't move.

I watch him and I wait *have to be sure* I will make sure *always make sure* and I do make sure and it's done.

His chest no longer rises.

I'm proud of you.

I smile.

So very, very proud.

I gush.

That's one out of three.

I've done it. I didn't fail you. Not this time.

I release him from me and his flaccid cock flops against his sticky pubic hair. I look down and I'm covered in blood. I look at him and he's covered in blood. I look at the walls and there are streaks of his blood across the wallpaper.

The room is bathed in red.

Don't worry about the room. Clean yourself up.

I start the shower and I stand under the water and I feel you behind me, wrapping your arms around me, keeping me safe, protecting me. You are Mrs Allen and you are Morosely Manor and you are me. We are all one. And we love each other. And we will do anything to spend eternity together.

I turn the heating up on the water until it won't turn up anymore. Steam fills the shower and my skin turns red but not blood-red so at least I'm being cleaned. You wash my hair and I close my eyes and feel your fingers between the strands.

You are Mrs Allen. You are Morosely Manor. You are me.

You kiss my neck. You tell me we'll always be together. Then you tell me Tilly has finished downstairs, and she's about to come up, so I need to get out of the shower and get dressed and dry my hair.

I get out the shower. Dry my body. Blow dry my hair. Dress myself in your clothes, the ones you kindly gave me, the ones that you approve of.

You are Mrs Allen. You are Morosely Manor. You are me.

And I love you.

Knock knock knock.

Tilly's waiting.

I put on a smile and I open the door, just enough to see the face of my daughter, and I can't wait to make her part of Morosely Manor too.

CHAPTER THIRTY-FIVE

Tilly doesn't feel safe around Mum anymore.

She feels safe around Dad.

Dad knows that Mum bruised her arm. He knows she grabbed her. He knows that there's something wrong.

So she knows she's safe when Dad is around.

So where is he?

Why isn't he in his office?

When she went to look inside, to say that she and Jack have finished work – where was he then?

And why was the bedroom door closed?

He must be inside. So she creeps to the door, puts her ear against it, and doesn't hear any keys tapping, or him speaking on the phone; just shuffling around.

She knocks.

A few seconds go by.

The door creaks open. Mum's pale face appears in the crack. She smiles.

That strange smile again…

A shiver runs from the top of Tilly's spine to the tip of her toes.

"Hello, darling, are you okay?"

"Yeah. Where's Dad?"

Mum doesn't answer straight away. She turns away and looks at something. Something in the room. Then turns back.

"Dad's not feeling well," she says.

"Can I see him?"

"I'm afraid not. Have you finished your work?"

Tilly nods.

"Well then why don't you go downstairs and sit in the living room? We'll watch the press conference together. I hear Boris is back. Won't that be exciting?"

Tilly doesn't really care about Boris or the press conference. She only watches them because they do it as a family. In truth, the look on Mum's face appears even more alien, and it's scaring her, and she wants Dad.

"Can I just see if Dad's okay?"

"We think he has the virus, darling. He needs to be quarantined. Needs to stay away from you, so you don't catch it. Do you understand?"

"But I–"

Mum lifts her arm back and pounds her fist into the wall. It makes Tilly jump.

"What part of *no* do you not understand, you wretched little ingrate?"

Tilly doesn't understand those words. She backs away.

"Dad?" she calls out.

Mum punches the wall again.

"I said he's fucking *ill*!"

She swings the door open and stands in the doorway. She seems to fill it. Her silhouette blocks out the light. The morphed features of her face twist and contort and this does not look like Mum anymore.

Tilly backs away.

"I told you to go downstairs and wait in the living room you insolent little beggar."

Mum steps out of the room. Toward Tilly.

Tilly backs away again.

"I am going to teach you not to disobey your parents, you ungrateful morsel, do you understand?"

"Yes, Mum."

"The word is *sorry*."

"Sorry, Mum."

"Now do as I say."

Tilly has tears in her eyes. She wills them away.

Mum raises her eyebrows.

"Yes, Mum," Tilly says. "Sorry, Mum."

Tilly turns around and runs away.

The bedroom door slams behind her.

She runs down the stairs, through the hallway, through the living room, into the kitchen and throws her arms around her brother.

She wants Dad. She *needs* Dad. She's trapped here and Mum is going crazy and Jack doesn't have a clue and Dad is the only one who can save her.

Without him, she is truly helpless.

CHAPTER THIRTY-SIX

"I am so sorry not to have been part of this trio for so long," says Boris. "I want to thank everybody who has been doing such a good job in my absence and I want to thank the NHS for so much; including getting me back here and I might add for a much happier hospital visit yesterday."

Who should go first?

"Across this country, therefore, families every day are continuing to lose loved ones before their time. We grieve for them and with them, but as we grieve we are strengthened in our resolve to defeat this virus."

Tilly is the biggest pest. The one who causes the most fuss. It might make sense to get her out of the way so she can't cause any more trouble.

"We are throwing everything at it, heart and soul, night and day, to get it right – and we will get it right and we are making huge progress."

Then again, Jack is the boy. He is stronger than Tilly, though not by much. He is the one who could put up the biggest fight. But he's a child, and I killed his father, so how much of a threat could he be?

"They are rising to a challenge we have never seen in our lifetimes, and the same can be said of the entire people in this country – staying in enforced confinement, not seeing family, not seeing friends or grandchildren, worrying about their jobs and the future."

Tilly is smarter. Jack is an idiot. She might catch onto what we plan first.

"And so I can confirm today that we are past the peak of this disease. We are past the peak and we are on the downward slope."

The well calls to me. I need to choose. I need to hurry. We want it done today. We will not waste any more time.

"We have come through the peak, or rather, we've come under what could have been a vast peak as though we've been going through some huge alpine tunnel and we can now see the sunlight and pasture ahead of us."

If Tilly ran she'd have nowhere to go. But I do not wish to chase. Please, tell me, which I should dispose of first. Or whether I should manage them both together...

"And so it is vital that we do not now lose control and run slap into a second and even bigger mountain."

...eeny meeny miny mo...

"I know we can do it, because we did it, and we've shown we can do it."

...catch a squirmer by its toe...

"The country came together in a way few of us have seen in our lifetimes."

...if it squeals, push it harder...

"To protect the NHS and to save lives and that's why I am absolutely convinced we can do it in phase two as well."

I stand.

"Can we play the video now."

I turn to Tilly.

"Stay here," I tell her.

I turn to Jack.

"Come with me."

"Where are we going, Mum?"

"You'll see."

I hold out my hand. He takes it. We walk through the living room.

"Jack, don't go!" Tilly says in a whispered shout.

He frowns at her.

Why wouldn't he go? I'm his mother.

"Forgive her," I say. "For she knows not what she does."

And I take him through the kitchen and into the garden.

It's raining and he's hesitant but I tell him it's okay and we walk into the storm.

"Are we going far, Mum?"

I see the well. I walk toward it and it sees me too.

"Not far, my darling," I tell him. "Not far at all."

CHAPTER THIRTY-SEVEN

Tilly rushes to the garden door. She presses herself against it, watching Jack being led by Mum's hand. She talks to him, nurtures him, grooms him, and he has no sense of danger at all.

But why should he? It's Mum.

She won't hurt them.

Would she?

Tilly looks at her arm. Scans the faint grey outline of her bruise.

She needs Dad. He was so concerned when he saw her arm. He finally caught a glimpse of the side of Mum that Tilly had feared for so long.

Mum had said not to disturb Dad. That he is unwell. That he is contagious. That he does not wish to infect the family.

Fine. In that case, Tilly would talk to him from the other side of the door. Surely germs can't get through a door?

Jack and Mum are halfway to the well. She has to hurry. She has no idea why, she just knows that something terrible is about to happen.

She sprints to the stairs, leaps up them two at a time,

scarpers across the hallway and pauses outside her parent's room.

She listens. Waits for movement. For the sound of Dad's breathing. Some indication that he is there.

But all she receives is silence.

She knocks gently on the door.

No response.

She knocks a little harder.

Still no response.

"Dad?"

Silence.

"Dad, are you there?"

Silence.

"Dad, please wake up. I need you."

Silence.

She glances over her shoulder. At the stairs. The route to her brother. How much time does she have?

She knocks more forcefully, and says with more assertion, "Dad, please wake up!"

Still, nothing.

Even this far into the house, she can hear the rain battering the old bricks of Morosely Manor. It's torrential, and it's becoming even more so, like God's attacking them, like the weather wants to condemn their home to solitude forever and ever.

And Jack is outside in it. Walking toward the overflowing well.

She bangs harder on the door.

"Dad, please!"

Still, her father does not respond.

Should she go in?

She places a hand on the door handle. Thinks twice. Then thinks again. She needs him. But he doesn't want to infect her. He always puts her first.

"Dad, I really need your help…"

Still silence.

"I'm coming in."

She takes a deep breath. Makes a decision. One she never normally takes; to go against her parent's wishes.

She turns the door handle. Pushes the door open, just a smidge.

"Dad?"

Lightning flashes outside the far window. From the narrow gap in the door, she can see Dad's foot on the bed. She peers a little further in, and she can see his leg. His trousers are around his ankles.

"Dad?"

He doesn't move.

The sheets are soaked in red.

She didn't notice it before, but now it's all she can see.

Is it blood?

What else would it be?

She doesn't want to enter, but she knows she must.

Dad isn't sick.

Mum is lying to her.

And Dad is…

She enters. Creeps. Inches into the room.

She sees his leg. His waist. His penis. Drenched in red gunk. It doesn't glisten in the flashing light; it isn't wet anymore. It's crusted.

She's crying, but she doesn't realise it.

She steps in and she sees his face.

His face.

What is wrong with his face…

His eyes. Open. Staring. At the ceiling. Mouth open.

And his neck…

A large, hacked-at wound, gaping at her, muscle sticking

out and bone sticking out and muscle sticking out and oh no Dad oh Dad oh Dad oh Dad…

She doesn't move. Not for a little while. Her body is rooted to the floor.

Then she screams and covers her own mouth to stop herself.

She runs out of the room. She can't look at it anymore. She rushes into the bathroom, locks herself in, crawls into the corner beneath the sink, wraps her arms around her legs and huddles them close to her and makes herself as small as she can and rocks, rocks, just keeps rocking.

Did Mum do that?

She wipes away tears.

Of course Mum did that.

Is he dead?

Of course he's dead.

Why was there so much blood?

She cries. It's all she can do. Cry. The image repeats itself over and over and, although she has no idea now, this is a moment of trauma that will revisit her for years to come.

If she survives, that is.

What if Mum hurts her too?

What is she about to do with Jack?

She wants to save Jack but she can't stop thinking about Dad and Mum oh Mum her loving caring Mum she did this and she needs to save Jack but Dad is dead he's dead he's dead and he's covered in blood did it hurt and why can't she stop seeing it please stop seeing it PLEASE STOP.

She covers her ears. Closes her eyes. Buries herself away.

Maybe she'll wake up.

But she won't wake up. You have to be asleep to wake up.

But Jack…

She needs to get Jack and run. There's no one around for

miles, but if they keep running, then they have to find someone eventually.

What if Mum chases them?

Oh, God, Jack…

He's so small. He's so clueless.

But he's her twin.

She pushes herself to her feet. Opens the door. Stares down the stairs.

She has no choice.

She has to go back for him.

She has to.

She glances at her parent's room. Her body seizes with terror. Her arms are shaking. She can barely walk, her feet are wobbling so much.

But she has to get to Jack.

And she has to get to him now.

CHAPTER THIRTY-EIGHT

My grip loosens the more cooperative he is.
He's not like Tilly.

He's a good boy.

He's a stupid boy.

Sometimes stupid means more obedient. Sometimes it's good not to have a smart child. Less inquisitive means they ask fewer questions.

And if he does ask questions, he's always satisfied with the answers he gets.

"Why are we in the rain, Mummy?"

"Because I want to show you something."

"Okay then."

I am drenched and he is drenched and although I know he's uncomfortable I am not. I am focussed. He is in one hand and I feel you in the other, leading me, guiding me, taking me to the well.

Water runs down its sides, crashing and splashing and running down the brick and into the grass so the mud sinks further beneath my feet.

Jack is wearing socks. He didn't even think to put shoes on, he just did as I said.

Good boy, Jack.

Stupid boy, Jack.

We reach the well. We stop. I let go of him and he doesn't run. He stays with me, staring up at me, waiting for me to explain why we are here.

I look at him. His hair is soaked and water dribbles down his face and he blinks it out of his eyes and keeps staring at me.

"Follow me, Jack."

You take my hand and you guide me onto the bricked surface surrounding the well. It is still wet but not grubby. It is damp but not slippery. It is rough on the sole of my feet.

"Come, Jack," I say, and Jack follows. He steps onto the brick and stands next to me.

"Look," I tell him, and I peer over the well.

He looks.

"What is it, Mummy?" he asks. "I can't see anything."

"Look closer."

He looks closer, peers into the water, and finally he can see it too. Deep in the well, wavy lines around his face, the dense water disguising his features. A boy. Jack's age. Looking up at us.

"Who's that, Mummy?"

"That's Billy."

"Who's Billy?"

"He belongs to the house too. He's going to be your friend."

You tell me I am doing well and I thank you.

You always tell me to be wary of Billy. He wasn't what you thought he would be. He received just punishment for his insolence. He is where children deserved to be.

He is a wretch. A fool. A delinquent. And all children must be punished.

I watch Jack. He still peers in. You tell me to look at the back of his head so I do. You tell me that's where my hand needs to be. I need to grab his hair, be forceful, and hold him under long after he stops squirming.

"Is he real, Mummy?"

"As real as you or I."

You tell me it is time, and I understand.

I take a step toward Jack, close enough that our bodies are touching. I stretch my arm. Flex my muscle. He's a child but he's going to fight once death is imminent. He may not mean to, but it is his body's instinct, and I need to be strong.

Just as I think *this is it,* just as I say *goodbye my boy*, as I say *I will see you very, very soon,* the insolence of another child shows me exactly why these children deserve to experience the pain that will make us part of this house.

"Jack!"

My head shoots around. It's Tilly. Stood ten or so paces away. Staring at us. Soaked. Young. Pathetic.

Jack turns and looks at her.

"Jack, come here!" she cries.

Jack doesn't move.

"Jack, please!"

"What are you doing, Tilly?" I ask.

She doesn't look at me, she just keeps beseeching Jack to "come here!"

"Do not move," I tell my son.

"Jack, it's not safe!"

"What do you mean it's not safe?" he asks, and he's a good boy, a stupid boy.

"Mum is not safe."

"What do you mean, Mummy is not safe?"

"I mean that – she's going to hurt you."

"Mummy would never hurt us."

"Yes, she would – she killed Dad!"

My face contorts into a snarl and I hate this child for bringing such disobedience to this wonderful moment.

"Stop lying!" Jack says. "You're always lying, always teasing me, and I don't like it."

Good boy. Stupid boy.

"I am not lying this time!"

I grin. I don't know what I was worried about. This girl is so unhinged that there is no way she could ever out-think us.

I will enjoy her death far more than Jack's.

"She's a monster!" she says. "She's a horrible person, she's not Mum!"

I grow angry. How dare she. How fucking dare she. I am not Mum? I am a monster? We are not monsters. We are Morosely Manor. We are the law. We are the mother.

And we are not happy.

"Please, Jack, just–"

"Tilly," I say. "Come here."

"No."

"I said come here, Tilly."

"No, I will not!"

This child has no respect, no manners, she is nothing like good boy stupid boy, she thinks she's smart, thinks she's better than us.

She is not better than us.

You assure me of that.

She will not outwit us. Not lure Jack away. And there is only one way to make her come closer.

"Very well," I say.

"Jack, come here!"

Before she can protest any longer, I take hold of the back of Jack's hair, ensuring I have a good grip of his head. He says "ow!" and "what are you doing?" but we ignore him and I pull his head back then plunge it into the well, under the water's surface, and I hold it there.

A few water bubbles rise. His body thrashes.

But we are far, far too strong for him.

CHAPTER THIRTY-NINE

Jack...

His body thrashes and protests and does all it can but it cannot overpower Mum.

She is stronger than she should be. Stronger by far. She has the power of two, and Tilly can't understand how, but if she doesn't do something soon, Mum will kill him.

But what?

What is she supposed to do?

She is a child. What can a child ever do?

"Stop!" she said. "Please!"

Mum looks back and grins at her and she has never seen that grin on Mum's face before and now she understands, she finally understands – that is not her mum.

That is not the woman who dabs her eyes when she cries or who raised her or who took her for walks back when they lived in London.

That is not the mother who taught her to read or taught her to ride her bike or taught her how to use her iPad.

Mum is not the crazy person who's hunting her children or muttering to herself or obsessing over this well.

It is this house. Something in it. Something doing this to her, making her act in this way, and maybe, just maybe, if she could find Mum again, Mum would stop what she's doing and come back to them.

"I love you, Mum," Tilly said.

Mum snorts a laugh.

"Really, I do. I know this isn't you."

Mum frowns.

"You need to fight, Mum."

She shakes her head. Mutters something to someone and turns back to the water.

Then her eyes widen. She sees something in the water. She looks scared.

The water bursts upwards. A large upward splash pushes both Mum and Jack up and onto the grass. Something from within the well rises out of it, something with force, something that packed a punch.

But what was it?

Jack sits up. Coughs. He's drenched but Tilly can still see his tears.

"Tilly…"

He runs to his sister and they wrap their arms around each other and they look back at Mum pushing herself slowly to her knees, muttering "That damn boy that insolent boy that horrible boy."

At first, Tilly thinks she's talking about Jack.

Then she says, "He's just as bad now as he was before."

Just like before? Before what?

Mum stands and turns toward her children, a look on her face that can only be interpreted as rage, and readies herself to charge at them, but there's another burst of water from the well and something comes out – some*one* comes out – and this some*one* smacks into the back of Mum and knocks her to the ground.

Then he pauses before them. A child. A boy. Their age. Dressed like they dressed a long time ago.

"Who are you?" Tilly asks.

"I'm Billy," he says. "Now *run*."

CHAPTER FORTY

I cough up water and I cannot believe this child, this damn child, this product of the devil, just as he was eighty years ago, cocky and pathetic, a mother's smothered wreck, showing up on my door without any knowledge of life or hard work or what it takes to be a man.

"What are you doing, Billy?" I say.

My voice has changed. It's different. Older. Well-spoken.

I am here but I am not myself. I don't know who I am, but something has taken over me. Is it you? Are you in me? Are you still pulling my strings?

You shush me and I sit back down as you stand up and you turn toward this ghostly figure, this apparition hovering before me, wearing the exact same attire as he did when I killed him.

"You wretch."

"Is that the best you can do?" he asks. "After all this time, that's all you can muster?"

"You won't win."

"Win? Win what? What am I winning?"

"You're a ghost. Transparent. You have no form. I have this woman."

"What you're doing to her is wrong."

"No, Billy. You're wrong. Now get out of my way."

I charge forward and I am covered in mud and my legs are heavy and I hate this body and I hate these clothes but Morosely Manor is my home and I will do as it wishes.

"You will not hurt them," Billy claims, stubbornly at my side, trailing me, following me.

I ignore him.

"I won't let you," he says.

It's such a long walk across this garden and the well will have these children, it will, it calls to me and it will.

"Morosely Manor doesn't deserve this family," he says.

I stop. Turn. Jab my finger at this impudent, audacious toad.

"Morosely Manor deserves whatever it wishes to have," I tell him. "And you would do well to respect it."

"I will stand between you and them."

"I have a body. I can hold a weapon, I can grab the children. You can push me away from a well and that's it. Until you have a body to command, you are nothing, so please, tell me, what exactly is it you will do?"

"Whatever I have to."

I can't help but laugh. He's grown up a lot in 81 years, but he's still in the body of a child, the face of an ingrate. And he's still an idiot who fails to recognise the pull of Morosely Manor; the sanctity of its walls, the love it provides those who fall into it. I am doing a service to this family, providing them with a forever home, with something they can belong to.

Billy is just a presence lurking in its walls, watching helplessly and talking too much.

"Why are you like this?" he asks.

I shake my head. I won't listen to this. I have things to do.

I charge across the garden.

"I just want to know – what happened to make you such a horrible old hag?"

"Children like you, Billy. Children like you. Now leave me be."

He seems to listen, as he disappears. Fades into the rain, and my head is clear, and I think again.

The children are in the house. Morosely Manor will not let them escape. It will trap them for me.

All I have to do now is find them.

CHAPTER FORTY-ONE

Tilly runs, hand gripped on Jack's arm, from the kitchen to the living room to the hallway – from one room to another, only to find the house fighting back.

She reaches the front door, takes hold of the handle, pulls on it, but the door won't budge. It's locked. Which is strange – Mum and Dad never lock it.

The key is on a hook above the door. Tilly leaps upwards but, just as she's about to reach it, it moves out of her grasp and soars across the room.

She lets go of Jack and chases it, into the bathroom, and screams as the key falls into the toilet bowl and the toilet flushes.

She returns to the door and pulls on it again.

Jack is crying. Standing in the middle of the room, his hands dropped by his sides, bawling his eyes out.

Tilly rushes up to him, grabs his hand, and says, "Jack, please stop crying."

She wipes the tears out of his eyes and looks into them, deep into them.

"We need to think, so please, stop crying."

He still sobs, but he stops wailing. That's probably the best she's going to get.

Mum's voice carries across the garden and into the house. She's arguing. Who with, Tilly doesn't know, but they can't wait here. If the house won't let them escape, then they will have to hide, so she grabs Jack's arm.

She rushes to the study, and the door slams in her way.

She doesn't have time to wonder how it slams of its own accord; she only has time to run. So she pulls Jack toward the bathroom, perhaps they could lock themselves in there – but that door shuts too.

The rain batters against the manor house and the wood creaks and moans and groans as she looks from the walls to the beams to the floor and wonders, terrified, where on earth they could go.

She turns to the stairs and sprints up the steps. From the upstairs hallway, she looks into the garden and sees Mum, still arguing. They have time. A bit of it. Enough time to hide.

She rushes towards the bathroom and the door shuts.

She rushes towards her bedroom and the door shuts.

Jack's room. Shuts.

Spare room. Shuts.

Even the room where Dad lies. Shuts.

Every single door shuts.

And she tries the handles, she barges into them, she kicks them, but they do not budge, and Jack is crying again and she does not know what to do.

She looks out the window. Mum finishes her argument. She walks toward the house.

Tilly looks around. They can't stay here. They are trapped with nowhere to go, so she pulls Jack back to the stairs, and they rush down, only to find every door downstairs close, and she is unable to open any of them.

All doors except the one that leads to the living room, then the kitchen, then the garden.

Mum's heavy footsteps enter the kitchen, stomping over the muddy prints left by her and her brother.

Tilly looks around. There is nowhere to go. Nowhere to run. Nowhere to turn to. The house has them trapped.

She tries the front door again, but the handle won't turn. She barges against it but it does not yield. Pounds and screams and begs and pleads but no one can hear them.

She grabs the hat stand and throws it at the window. but the hat stand resists, deviating from its course and turning back to Tilly, knocking her and Jack over.

Mum's footsteps in the living room.

Tilly stands.

Mum's footsteps in the hallway.

Pulls Jack up.

Mum's footsteps stopping.

And they are alone. Nowhere to run. With the one person who should save them, but is not willing to let them go.

Morosely Manor will not let them go.

And Tilly knows she has lost.

CHAPTER FORTY-TWO

They wait for me.

Maybe they understand. Maybe they see how loving Morosely Manor is, how nurturing it is, how safe they will be residing here with us. People will come and go, but we will remain, and we will love each other and we will love it.

It's the most peaceful alternative to death.

I step toward them. They back away. Clinging to each other. Shaking.

"Why are you so afraid?" I say. "I've lived in this house since I was a little girl, and it's always kept me safe."

They cower. He cries. She stares. Stupid boy good boy and insolent little brat.

"Come here," I tell them, softening my voice, showing them that I come with love. "Come on."

They back away until they meet a wall and have nowhere to go. I approach, reach my hand out, and graze the back of my knuckles down his damp cheek.

"You're so wet," I say. "So, so wet."

And I turn to her. Even though she has caused me so much trouble, the house still wants her.

We still want her.

"And you…" I stroke my fingers down her cheek. She recoils. "It's quick. So quick. You'll barely feel a thing."

She says nothing. Her lips are tight, like she's trying not to cry.

I wish they would stop crying. Stop being so scared. This is a happy moment, and they are running the risk of ruining it.

"You don't understand now," I tell them. "But you will. Oh, you will. Once you are a part of this house…"

"I don't want to be a part of this house," Tilly says. Her voice is small and uncertain, but with a distant tone of confidence. I wish Lisa had done better in raising the girl.

"Whyever not?"

"Because it's a house. I'm a girl. I don't want to die."

"Oh, my dear, it's not just a house. And you won't be just a girl. And you'll never die. You'll be with me. With us. With Daddy. Wouldn't you like to be with Daddy?"

Her frown refuses to yield.

I turn to the boy.

"Your father is part of the house now," I tell him. "I made it so."

The boy says nothing. Perhaps he doesn't know.

"Hasn't she told you?" I tut at Tilly. "Silly girl. Holding back the truth is the same as lying, you know."

"Don't listen to her, Jack."

"Who do you trust, Jack? The lying brat? Or your mother?"

"You're not our mother," Tilly interjects.

"Do not talk back to me!" I snap. Now I am starting to get angry. "Your mother is in here with me and she knows what's best for you."

Tilly grips her brother's hand.

Why doesn't he say anything?

"I've had enough of this. You will follow me to the well."

"We will not!"

I slap her across the cheek, hard, Lisa's wedding ring leaving an indent in her cheek. When she looks back at me, she's shocked.

"Now I know you're not Mum," she says.

I look at Jack. He's quieter. He seems to be understanding.

Yet he still does not speak.

"This way," I say, and I turn, expecting them to follow, and they do.

And then the boy speaks.

Except, when he speaks, it is not his voice. It is another's voice. A voice I know well.

And it tells me, "No, Mrs Allen."

I turn to look at him, aghast.

"You will not hurt anyone else," says Billy.

CHAPTER FORTY-THREE

Tilly looks from Mum to Jack.

Except, it isn't Mum or Jack anymore.

At least, it may be them in body, but it isn't them, not really. She isn't sure how it's happened, but when she looks at their faces, she no longer sees their faces.

In Mum, she sees an old lady. Chaotic grey hair. Old lady clothes. A face that looks like it's incapable of smiling.

In Jack, she sees another boy. Their age. Maybe a little younger. He's wearing a cap. Shorts. Brown shoes. Grey socks. A brown, sleeveless jumper. A lighter brown shirt.

In fact, he looks exactly like those pictures of World War Two evacuees she saw in her history lesson at school.

And his name is Billy.

For a moment, they say nothing. The shock sits between them, festering. Billy has a look of determination, a look of defiance. His arms shake but he stands tall, refusing to back down despite his obvious terror.

Mrs Allen hunches over. Her face contorts between one expression of rage to another, too outraged to form words.

She shakes her head, and says, quietly, "Oh, Billy… You incompetent fool…"

"No, Mrs Allen," Billy insists, trying to hide the shake of his voice. "I am not incompetent. I am not a fool."

"Yes, you are."

"No I am not."

"You are an impudent little wretch, a delinquent, a disgusting piece of filth!"

"No, I am not! I am not impudent, I am not a wretch, I am not a delinquent, and I am not disgusting!"

"Why you little–"

"But you are, Mrs Allen." He shakes his head. Bites his lip. Seems to grow stronger, somehow. "You are."

Her eyebrows lift. Her lip quivers. She tries to form words, but he beats her to it.

"You are insolent. You are wretched. And you are, without a doubt, disgusting."

"How dare you–"

"And you will not take this family. Not like you took me from mine."

"I gave you eternity."

"You stole my childhood."

"I am giving this family–"

"An eternity stuck in an old house with *you*." He steps toward her. "And I assure you, Mrs Allen, that is far from a perfect afterlife."

"You were always such a horrible little vagabond, and your mother–"

"My mother loved me, Mrs Allen. Just like the mother you're stealing right now loves these children. And it is *you* who is horrible."

He steps toward her again.

"You–"

"No, Mrs Allen. Your words don't hurt me anymore. And

what else can you do? You've already killed me."

"I gave you–"

"Nothing, Mrs Allen!" He steps toward her and he is really close to her, staring her in the face, glaring at her with all the hatred he has accumulated over decades of despair. "You gave me *nothing.*"

She lifts her hand out and goes to strike him, but he catches the arm, and he sinks his fingers into it, and he looks her dead in the eyes.

"You will let this family go," he tells her.

"It is Morosely Manor that–"

"Then this house will let them go!"

She shakes her head. But something is changing. Something in her face. There is a flicker of Mum, then it changes back, it returns to Mrs Allen.

But he's winning.

Billy is winning.

"You wretched little–"

"You hurt me."

"Why I ought to–"

"And my mother never even knew where to look for me."

"You ungrateful–"

"And while I am stuck here with you forever, I will not let anyone else face such an eternity of hell."

Mum.

Tilly can see her.

Behind the eyes, behind the anger there is a vulnerability, and she sees it, and she steps forward, and she places a hand on her mother's arm, and she says, "Mum?"

Mrs Allen pushes the arm away.

"Don't stop, Tilly," Billy tells her, and Tilly puts her arm on Mum's arm again.

"I'm here, Mum."

"Stop it!"

"I'm here."

"I said stop it!"

"And I'm not going anywhere."

The snarls turn into tears turn into anger turn into suffering turn into… Mum.

And Billy turns to me.

"Now go," he says. "Before she comes back."

Then Billy is gone.

CHAPTER FORTY-FOUR

At first, I do not know where I am.

I was in here somewhere. Roaming the halls, dawdling around the corridors, listening to everything you said, but now I know.

I know.

You do not guide me anymore.

And I see my children. My dear, dear children.

And I remember…

I was going to drown them. Oh, God, I was going to drown them.

I put my arms around them and take them to our knees and we hold each other, we cry together, and I killed Adam, oh God, I killed Adam…

But it's not over.

The house calls to me.

I can hear it. It has dug its claws into my mind and it will not release it.

It's too late for me.

"Mum," Tilly says, wiping her tears and looking up at me. "Mum, we have to go. Billy said we have to go."

I look to the door.

"Then go," I tell her, and I take keys from my pocket and put them in her hand.

Tilly grabs my hand and stands but, in her rush to the door, her fingers lose their grasp of my fingers, and she pauses, looking back at me.

"Mum?" she says. "Come on."

I am still here, Lisa... Inside of you...

I bow my head. Wipe my eyes. Stop crying. Stop showing pain. I have to show strength to my children. I have shown them weakness for so long, now I must show them strength.

"I am not coming," I say.

Stop them from leaving, or I will gut you...

I go to grab them, pull them back in the house, take them to the well, then get a hold of myself.

If they stay any longer, I am scared for what I might do.

"Mum! You have to come!"

I look from Tilly's face to Jack's. She's always so strong. He's always so content. I have two remarkable children, and I hate saying goodbye to them.

"Leave," I tell them. "Run, and do not stop running until you find someone, then tell them to call the police."

"I'm not–"

"Now, Tilly. I will not ask twice."

Kill them... Kill them before they get away...

My attempt to sound assertive fails. I can't let them know they won't see me again. I can't, or they will never go.

"But Mum–"

"I'll be right here. I promise. I'll hold them off so you can get away, then you can get help, and you can come back here, and you can save me."

Tilly looks into my eyes. I am sure a part of her knows I am lying, but she accepts it, and she takes her brothers hand, and they rush to the door.

Stop them!

I run after them ready to dig my fingers into their skin and pull them back and drown them in the well the well the well–

And I stop myself.

I must stop myself.

They unlock the door. Open it. Turn back to me.

"I love you," Tilly says.

"I love you as well, Mummy," Jack says.

They know.

Oh God, they know.

They don't realise they know, but they know.

This is goodbye.

"I love you too."

And they leave.

Go after them! Get them! Kill them!

Defiant, I turn.

They will run, and they will find the police, and they will come back.

But Lisa knows that, when they return, they will find nothing of the house they left.

She strides through the kitchen.

You idiot, go get them!

Opens the drawer.

I said get them!

Takes out a box of matches.

What are you doing?

Lights one. Throws it to the corner.

I will kill you myself...

How? How will you kill me? You're only as strong as the wooden beams that hold up this roof, and I'm about to show you how strong they are.

I light another match. Throw it at another corner.

Enter the living room. Light it. Throw it.

Enter the study. Light. Throw.

The bathroom. Light. Throw.

Upstairs. Light. Throw.

Light. Throw.

Light. Throw.

Light, throw, light, throw, light, throw, until Morosely Manor is ablaze with flames, and I am in the middle of it, watching the wooden beams crack and the stairs give way and all the possessions we moved with six weeks ago erupt.

And I make my way to the bedroom. Look down at the man I vowed to love, but forgot how to somewhere along the way.

I ignore the violence inflicted upon the body; close my eyes so I can't see it, and I lay down on the bed, place my arm across his chest, and fall asleep holding my husband in my arms.

It takes the children two hours and fifty-six minutes to reach the nearest houses. They run across fields, then go back on themselves, then repeat the same part of the fields, and get lost, and despair, until, eventually, they come across a small village of peculiar looking houses and pound on one of the doors.

An elderly couple answer and find a pair of grubby children. The children reminds them of when they were young, evacuated to the countryside during the war; where they met, fell in love, and lived together ever since.

They call the police, and the police arrive and take the children to the station before driving to Morosely Manor to find the mother and father the children would not stop talking about.

Only, when they arrive, they find a raging fire, and by the time the fire fighters manage to put it out, the house and its contents are nothing but rubble and ash.

They never do find my body.

But they do find the bones of a boy and a man at the bottom of the well.

A well that had somehow been left unaffected by the fire.

A well that remained the only thing left standing.

A well that was no longer overflowing, since the rain had stopped when the fire began.

TWENTY YEARS LATER

CHAPTER FORTY-FIVE

Harry drives his electric SUV around the corners of the country roads like he's never driven a car before. She can't help but smile. He's a city man, through and through, and the sight of a tractor coming toward him on such a small road just confuses him.

"Bloody imbecile," Harry mutters, quiet enough so that their daughters don't hear.

Matilda glances in the rear-view mirror. Her two daughters are impeccably behaved, despite the long and arduous journey from Edinburgh, and she's proud of them for being so quiet.

Harry, however, is slightly more disgruntled.

"I still don't understand," Harry protests. "We had our minutes silence for the coronavirus victims earlier this month. Why are we here?"

To be fair to him, she hasn't explained much about why they've come here. She told him it's to do with the impact of the virus, but that's a very small part of the truth, if it even is part of the truth at all. But, despite his protests, he's a loyal husband and he booked the time off work and put their daughters in the car and did as she asked.

Her mobile beeps. It's a text. Jack has arrived.

She puts her phone away and looks out of the windows. All fields look the same – at least, according to Harry – yet these fields look familiar. She remembers running over them, sweaty, despairing.

She likes to think of her mother doing the same, searching for them night after night, desperate to find the children she'd let go.

After all, they never found the body.

"We're here," Harry grunts, and turns the car down another path, one lined with trees, one that leads to…

Nothing.

Just a large patch of cement where a house once stood.

"What is this?" Harry asks as he brings the car to a halt.

Matilda smiles. Places a hand on her husband's leg, and says, "Wait here," then steps out of the car.

The trees seem to arch further over the driveway, yet the shadows are smaller than they used to be. She approaches the patch of land and sees a familiar figure in a suit, his shirt untucked and his top button undone.

"Hey," she says.

Jack turns around, runs up to her and takes her in his arms. He spins her around, saying, "Tilly, it's so good to see you! I can't believe it's been so long…"

Harry steps out of the car and approaches, frowning. He lets their daughters out, and they run across the fields as Harry strides toward them.

"Who's this?" Harry demands.

"My brother," Matilda says.

"Another foster brother?"

"No, Harry, this is my actual brother. This is Jack."

Jack holds out a hand. This seems to disarm Harry. They

shake hands, and it makes Matilda think back to a time when they wouldn't have been able to shake hands.

"Why are we here?" Harry asks.

Matilda turns back to the empty space where Morosely Manor used to be.

"This is where I used to live," she says.

"What? Here?"

"There was a house here once."

"You never mentioned–"

"Hey, Harry, could you watch the girls for me? Give me a minute with my brother?"

Harry looks warily from Matilda to Jack, probably wondering why he didn't know he was finally meeting her brother, after all these years, in the middle of nowhere. Still, he does as she asks, and he goes to find the girls.

"Seems nice," Jack says. "Take it you haven't told him much?"

"What would I tell him?"

Jack doesn't answer. He looks around. It's hot, and he removes his jacket.

"How was the flight?" she asks.

"Long."

"Is it much different in America?"

Jack shrugs. "Yes, on the one hand. Then, not different enough, on the other."

She smiles. Takes his hand and leans her head against his shoulder.

There is so much to say, but she can't articulate a word of it. So she lets the silence linger between them, and in the peacefulness of the afternoon, they let the matter rest.

"Come on," she says. "Let's get it over with."

They walk into the centre of the empty space and sit, cross legged, opposite each other. They take each other's hands, look down, and close their eyes.

She sighs. "What should I say?" she asks.

"I have no idea."

They laugh.

"Right, let me think…"

What should she say?

Would anyone even be listening?

She shakes herself out of it. Of course they would be.

"We just wanted to let you know," Matilda says. "That… we forgive you. After all this time, we…"

She feels tears. She wills them away.

"We miss you," Jack carries on. "And we forgive you. And we are fine. We just wanted to let you know that – we are fine."

"I have daughters. They remind me of you. They have your smile."

"And I didn't turn out to be as much of a screw-up as everyone thought I would."

They both chuckle.

A cool breeze brushes past them, prickling their skin, lifting the hair on their arms. It carries with it a whisper, a soft one, carrying delicate words that were meant just for them.

And then it leaves. And it's hot again. And they are done.

They open their eyes. Look at each other. Smile.

And Jack meets her daughters. Her husband. They have a meal together in a pub twenty or so minutes' drive away, stay at a hotel, then have breakfast the next day.

Matilda shares with her family the story of Morosely Manor, and they listen to every word.

Harry drops Jack off at the airport the next day. Jacks insists on going in alone, as they have a long journey back to Scotland. Matilda compromises – she walks him to the door, just so they can have a moment alone.

They spend that moment in silence, until they hear the call for a one-way flight to New York boarding.

"Don't leave it so long next time," she tells him.

"Maybe you can come visit me in New York someday."

"Yeah, sure. Someday."

Another silence lingers. They smile, and they hug, and Jack leaves, and as she waves, Matilda knows she'll never make it to New York.

She returns to the car and gazes out the window as they drive away from the south of England, away from the rural areas where both nothing and everything happens all at once.

She promises herself that she won't leave it so long to come back and visit, but she never comes back again, and the place where the home they inhabited for six long weeks once stood, eventually becomes something else. Another house, a safari, a walking site, it doesn't matter. It makes no difference to Matilda.

But she still visits Morosely Manor, if only in her dreams. Sometimes, city people like her husband wonder how a person can become attached to a house – something he says is just brick and mortar.

She doesn't explain it to him, as he doesn't understand.

And she dreams some more.

And she smiles.

And she is content.

And they never mention *Morosely Manor* again.

JOIN RICK WOOD'S READER'S GROUP...

And get **Roses Are Red So Is Your Blood** for free!

Join at **www.rickwoodwriter.com/sign-up**

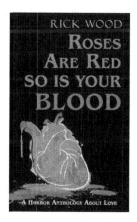

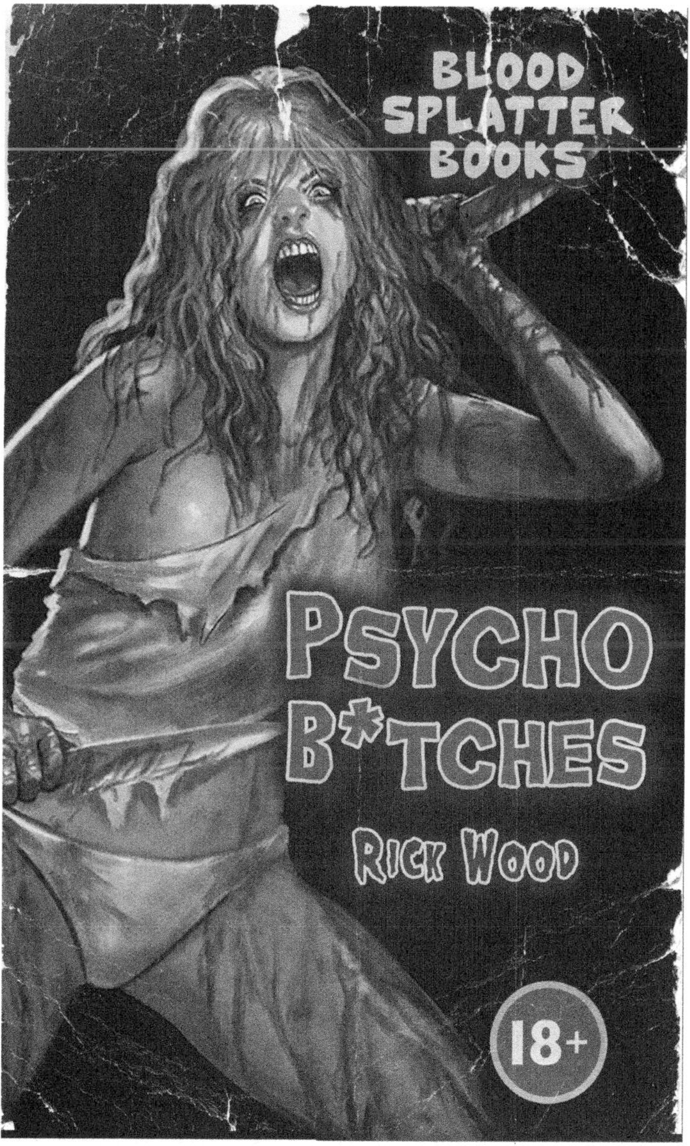
BLOOD
SPLATTER
BOOKS
PSYCHO
B*TCHES
RICK WOOD
18+

BLOOD
SPLATTER
BOOKS

THIS BOOK
IS FULL OF
BODIES

RICK WOOD

18+

BLOOD
SPLATTER
BOOKS

SHUTTER
HOUSE

RICK WOOD

18+

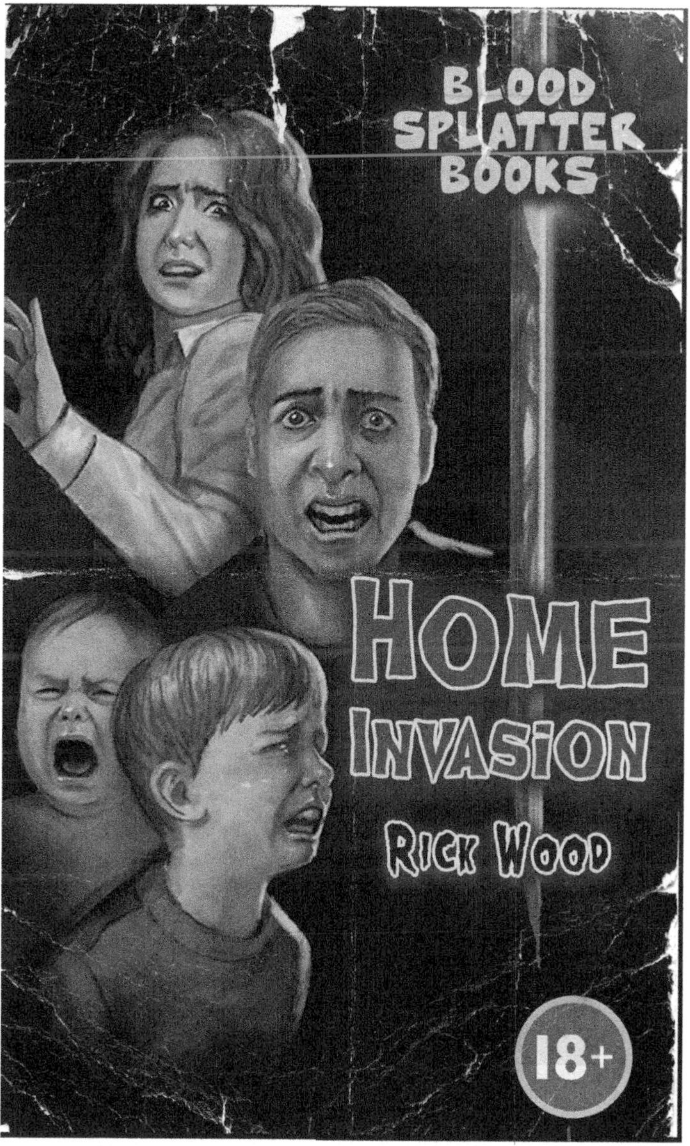
BLOOD
SPLATTER
BOOKS
HOME
INVASION
RICK WOOD
18+

BLOOD
SPLATTER
BOOKS

WOMAN
SCORNED

Rick Wood

18+

ALSO BY RICK WOOD...

THE
SENSITIVES

RICK WOOD

BOOK ONE IN THE ROGUE EXORCIST SERIES

THE HAUNTING OF EVIE MEYERS

RICK WOOD

Printed in Great Britain
by Amazon